Hi! My name is Dani and I'm the one who's crazy about football.

I'm a bit of a tomboy and sometimes people even mistake me for a boy! Lissa did on the first day of school, even though she denies it and says she was only joking.

You're probably wondering what someone like me is doing at Riverside Academy which is an all-girls' school. I wonder myself sometimes!

Actually, I won a sports scholarship here and now I love it. That's because I get to play netball and hockey. And I'm captain of the hockey team! And Mrs Waters, our PE teacher, thinks I'm the bee's knees! (Do bees have knees?)

But, best of all, I've got three brilliant friends called Lissa, Ali and Tash. The only trouble is I don't get to play football any more. Not at school anyway . . .

Chris Higgins

The Secrets Club

No Match for Dani

PUFFIN

PUFFIN BOOKS

Published by the Penguin Group
Penguin Books Ltd, 80 Strand, London WC2R ORL, England
Penguin Group (USA) Inc., 375 Hudson Street, New York, New York 10014, USA
Penguin Group (Canada), 90 Eglinton Avenue East, Suite 700, Toronto, Ontario,
Canada M4P 2Y3 (a division of Pearson Penguin Canada Inc.)
Penguin Ireland, 25 St Stephen's Green, Dublin 2, Ireland (a division of Penguin Books Ltd)
Penguin Group (Australia), 707 Collins Street, Melbourne, Victoria 3008, Australia
(a division of Pearson Australia Group Pty Ltd)
Penguin Books India Pvt Ltd, 11 Community Centre, Panchsheel Park,
New Delhi – 110 017, India
Penguin Group (NZ), 67 Apollo Drive, Rosedale, Auckland 0632, New Zealand
(a division of Pearson New Zealand Ltd)
Penguin Books (South Africa) (Pty) Ltd, Block D, Rosebank Office Park,
181 Jan Smuts Avenue, Parktown North, Gauteng 2193, South Africa

Penguin Books Ltd, Registered Offices: 80 Strand, London WC2R ORL, England

puffinbooks.com

First published 2013
001

Text copyright © Chris Higgins, 2013
Illustration of Dani copyright © Helen Huang, 2013
Chapter illustrations copyright © Puffin Books, 2013
All rights reserved

The moral right of the author and illustrator has been asserted

Typeset in 13.5 /17.5 Baskerville MT Std by Palimpsest Book Production Ltd,
Falkirk, Stirlingshire
Printed in Great Britain by Clays Ltd, St Ives plc

British Library Cataloguing in Publication Data
A CIP catalogue record for this book is available from the British Library

ISBN: 978-0-141-33524-7

www.greenpenguin.co.uk

MIX
Paper from
responsible sources
FSC® C018179

Penguin Books is committed to a sustainable
future for our business, our readers and our planet.
This book is made from Forest Stewardship
Council™ certified paper.

ALWAYS LEARNING   **PEARSON**

For all you lovely fans of the Secrets Club series

Chapter 1

'Guess what I'm doing tomorrow,' announces Tash at Friday lunchtime as we sit down at our favourite picnic bench next to the netball courts.

I slide in next to Lissa, saying, 'Budge up, Fatty.' It's OK, she knows it's a joke. Lissa's thin as a rake, even though she never stops eating. She's already scoffed her sandwiches and is now attacking a packet of crisps and eyeing my chocolate brownie enviously.

'Performing brain surgery?' she mumbles, spraying crisp crumbs all over me. 'Oops, sorry, Dan! D'you want that cake?'

'Going to the UN conference on climate control?' asks Ali, which is what she'd like to be doing. She and her nerdy mate Austen are on a mission to save the planet. He's at a different school from us because Riverside Academy for Girls doesn't take boys. Obviously.

Actually, he's not really nerdy; he's quite cool. Even though he doesn't like football.

'Playing in the centre for West Park Wanderers?' I ask as I smack Lissa's fingers away. 'Get off my cake!'

'Wrong!' Tash's eyes are sparkling. She's so pretty with her big smile and her hair plaited into hundreds of tiny braids, each with a blue or yellow bead on the end – school colours. Her mum does it for her.

'Meeting up with you!' she says, beaming, and Ali shrieks and flings her arms round her. We're all best mates, but Ali and Tash are super-extra best, if you know what I mean, so Ali was upset when she thought her bezzie didn't want to spend time with her at weekends. It turned out that Tash was looking after her mum who's got MS and her three little brothers and desperately trying to keep the whole family together, all on her own. Respect.

'Now we've got support at home I can catch up with you guys for a few hours,' she explains.

'Yay! I can feel a shopping fest coming on!' says Lissa.

'You've got enough clothes already!' says Ali who recycles everything.

'OK then, coffee and cake,' concedes Lissa happily. 'You coming, Dani?'

I hesitate.

'You've got to come!'

'I can't. I play football on Saturdays. You know that.'

'You don't have to . . .' says Lissa sulkily.

'Yes I do.'

Ali looks perplexed. 'But I thought you just went out and kicked a ball around with some mates.'

'You can do that anytime,' Tash points out. 'Come with us.'

'It's difficult. I don't want to let people down.'

'You're letting *us* down!' says Lissa, and everyone goes quiet. Then Ali, who likes to think things through properly, says, 'But . . . I don't get it. I mean, it's not like you play for a team, is it?'

They're all staring at me. Tash's eyes widen. 'You don't, do you?'

'No!'

This is the first time anyone has asked this question. I know why. Until now it's just been

3

Ali and Lissa meeting up together on Saturdays. Tash couldn't and I wouldn't. Simple. Only it's not quite as simple as that any more. Now that Tash is available, suddenly all the focus is on me.

'Of course I don't. It's just that . . .' I hesitate. Maybe now is the time to tell them. I've been wanting to for ages.

But if I do they'll want to come and watch me. And then everything could blow up in my face. I can't take the risk.

'It's just that you eat, sleep and breathe football and you'd rather do that than hang out with us,' says Lissa, and because she sounds so sour about it I decide I don't want to tell her any more.

'Please, Dani,' pleads Tash. 'It'll be a laugh, the four of us.'

'It won't be the same without you,' Ali points out. 'You're one of the gang.'

'The Gang of Four,' wheedles Tash.

'The No Secrets Club!' says Lissa. Then she adds, 'Unless you've got a secret, that is.'

'Cos if you have, you can't be in it,' teases Tash.

'That's rich coming from you!' I retort. 'And you!' I add, seeing Ali grinning.

4

'Come with us then!' persists Lissa. I roll my eyes and she sees it as surrender. 'Hurray!' she yells. 'We're all going to hang out together tomorrow. It's going to be brilliant! Now don't be late, you lot! Donatella's Coffee Shop at eleven.'

She is sooooo bossy.

Chapter 2

Saturday morning, on the train to Gran's, and I still haven't told my friends I'm not coming. I've put it off till I'm on my way because I know they'll try to change my mind.

Not that they'll succeed.

My sports bag is on the floor between my feet and I'm picking at the skin round my nails. Beside me my ten-year-old sister Jade has got her head stuck in a book as usual. She's only eighteen months younger than me but we're like chalk and cheese. I'm always doing something active, while Jade is permanently in a world of her own. If she's not reading stories she's making them up herself, scribbling them down in an exercise book which she carries with her everywhere.

I tug at a piece of skin but it resists and starts stinging so I stop peeling strips off myself as a delaying tactic and take out my phone. Quickly I scroll through my contacts till I come to NS Club. No Secrets. That's a joke. Who shall I ring to break the bad news? Not Tash – she'll ask too many questions; not Lissa – she'll go all moody on me; Ali's the safest bet.

'Hi, Dani!' Ali sounds puffed as if she's rushing. 'I'm on my way! Running a bit late cos my mum made me sort out my washing and tidy my room – I mean, I don't know what's wrong with her – she always does this on Saturday mornings – she's so annoying – anyway, I'll see you in fifteen –'

'I can't come,' I say, cutting her off mid-flow.

'Why not?' Her voice is shrill with disappointment. 'You're not playing football, are you?'

I really want to say yes and tell her all about it but now's not the time. Not in front of Jade.

'I've got to go and see my gran.'

'Daan-iiii!'

'I know! There's nothing I could do about it.

7

My mum said I had to. I'm on the train now with my sister. I'm really sorry.'

'It's OK.' Her tone is softer now, kinder. 'It's not your fault. Mums, eh?'

'Say sorry to the others for me, will you? I don't want them to think I've let them down.'

'I will. Don't worry, I'll explain.'

'Thanks, Ali. See you Monday.'

I switch off my phone and sigh with relief. That wasn't so bad after all. Beside me Jade says, without even glancing up from her book, 'You told a lie.'

'No I didn't. We *are* going to see Gran.'

'Not that. You said Mum said we had to.'

I glare at her as she turns the page. How can she do that, read a book and earwig my conversation at the same time?

'It's difficult. My friends all want to meet up together but I can't because now we go to Gran's every Saturday.'

'Yeah, but we don't *have* to. Mum doesn't *make* us. We're going because we want to.'

'I know that,' I say defensively.

'I like seeing Gran.'

'So do I!'

'So tell them then. Tell them the truth.'

It's annoying having a conversation with someone who's continuing to read a book at the same time but can still make sound observations and draw logical conclusions. Especially if she's eighteen months younger than you.

'It's not that simple.'

'Why not?'

'It's what we always do.'

'Not always. We never used to. Only since you started secondary school and Mum lets us go on the train on our own.'

'Exactly. It's become a habit. Gran expects to see us now every week. She looks forward to it.'

'Yeah! So do I. But Gran wouldn't hold you to it if you had something else to do. Neither would Mum. Mum's always telling you to get out and spend time with your new girl-mates.'

Suddenly she looks up at me with her wide, candid eyes. 'All I'm saying is no one is *forcing* you to go to see Gran. Not me, not Gran and certainly not Mum, so don't make out we are. If you want to stay home sometimes and meet

9

up with your friends, that's fine. OK? What's difficult about that?'

I stare at her furiously then resort to my usual clincher for winning an argument with my sister. 'You wouldn't understand. You're too young.'

Chapter 3

Gran lives alone in a bungalow on the edge of the small town of Blackett. It takes about an hour to get there. Blackett isn't the sort of place my friends would ever go to. It doesn't have enough of a High Street for Lissa or Tash and it's too environmentally unfriendly for Ali. Not enough green spaces. In fact, the only green spaces I can think of are the football pitch, where the local team Blackett United play, and the park alongside it. My dad used to play on that pitch. You can catch a glimpse of it down below out of Gran's front window.

Gran is Dad's mum. Dad is mad about football, like me. We used to go to watch West Park Wanderers together, just the two of us, and Jade stayed home with Mum because she was too little. It was ace. Mum used to joke that she should've called me Daniel instead of Danielle because Dad treated me like the son he never had.

We don't watch the Wanderers together any more though. Dad moved down south for work a few years ago and when he came back there was a really bad atmosphere in the house, and then last year he and Mum got divorced. Now he takes his new wife's sons with him to watch some rubbish local team instead.

I miss my dad.

Gran does too. That's one of the reasons I like going to see her. She's got photos of us all around her sitting room and he's in most of them, though in the most recent ones it's just him and Jade and me. We talk about him lots in her house and it makes me feel as if he's still here instead of miles and miles and miles away.

At home the only photos of Dad are in Jade's bedroom and mine. Mum doesn't mention Dad much, so neither do we in case it upsets her.

True to form Gran opens the door and announces, 'You just missed him on the phone. He says he'll call you later.'

Gran is small like me and her hair is cropped

short like mine too (though hers is iron-grey and mine's a sort of sandy colour) but that's where the resemblance ends. We have very different clothes sense. She favours long flowing skirts and layers of floaty tops and beads and rings and bangles, whereas I'm more of a jeans or tracky-pants kind of girl. We are similar in other ways though. Both of us are always on the go.

Gran used to be a teacher but she's retired now. From teaching that is, not from everything else. She's always swimming or playing tennis or badminton or golf, plus she belongs to a book group, she works in a charity shop and she's a school governor too. I get my sportiness from her. That's how I ended up at Riverside Academy for Girls.

When Gran first suggested I try out for Riverside I said, 'No way! I don't want to go to an all-girls' school!' But then we looked it up online and discovered it had a fantastic reputation for sport, so I agreed to sit the entrance test. Then, lo and behold, I ended up being offered the free sports scholarship and Mum and Gran persuaded me it would be a good idea to take it.

I'm glad I did. I thought it would be full of snobby posh girls who were really up themselves but it's not. Well, Lissa's posh, her family's really well off and her house looks like something out of a magazine, according to Ali who's been there for tea, but she's not a snob. She's mad about sport too and she's really good at hockey, though not as good as me. (It's the truth, I'm not boasting!) Everyone voted for me to be hockey captain, not her. It didn't stop us becoming good friends though, and we sit next to each other in class.

Tash and Ali sit in front of us. They're not posh at all. Tash lives in one of the tower blocks on the Borne Hill Estate and she won a scholarship too, an academic one cos she's dead brainy, though you wouldn't think it when you first meet her. She's into fashion mags and the celeb world. Ali lives in an ordinary house like ours, even though her sister really *is* a celebrity, and she's passionate about the environment. Neither Tash nor Ali is the slightest bit up themselves, though they've got loads to be big-headed about.

Actually, there are some real airheads at Riverside Academy, if I'm honest. Three spring to mind immediately, called Georgia, Zadie and Chantelle. They are totally obsessed with their appearance so I gave them a nickname straight away and the name stuck. Now everyone knows them as the Barbies and they're so stupid they think it's a compliment. They spread a rumour round, about Tash's mum being an alcoholic, because they saw her stumbling about in town. But now she's been diagnosed with MS, they're the ones who look pathetic.

I don't miss my old friends much. You see, they were mainly boys and I still kick a football around in the street with most of them because they live nearby. But the thing I really miss about my new secondary school is playing footie in a proper team. At my primary school I was the captain of the football team. But Riverside Academy for Girls doesn't play football.

'What's for lunch?' asks Jade, sniffing appreciatively. Gran always cooks us something nice to eat, another good reason for going to see her every week.

'Thai green curry, a new recipe. It's ready when you are.'

My mouth is watering. But I say, 'Mind if I have mine a bit later, Gran?'

She laughs. 'Go on then!' she says. 'It can wait. You're just like your father was, always itching to be outside in the fresh air. Go and run some of that energy off in the park and don't come back till you've built up an appetite.' Gran turns to Jade. 'I picked up a couple of books for you this week that someone brought into the shop. Do you want them now or after lunch?'

'Now!' says Jade, her eyes shining, and they disappear into the house together in search of magic and mystery. How can two sisters be so different?

'See you later!' I shout, hitching my bag back on to my shoulder, and set off down the hill. At the bottom there's a public loo and I nip inside. I take a hoody from my bag and pull it on over my T-shirt and tracksuit bottoms, staring at myself thoughtfully in the mirror.

I look like a boy.

'Hi,' I say to my reflection in my normal voice. I take a deep breath, square my shoulders, tuck my chin in and try again.

'Hiya!' My voice is deeper now and carries more. I cough and clear my throat and drop another octave.

'All right?' I say to the mirror and now my voice is husky, almost gravelly.

I can even sound like a boy if I try.

A woman comes in, looks at me startled, and scuttles into a cubicle. She must wonder what on earth this crazy guy is doing in the Ladies, talking to himself. I grin wryly at myself and then glance at my watch.

Time to go.

Chapter 4

'Where did you get that bruise from?' squeals Georgia. My heart sinks.

'OMG!' Zadie's and Chantelle's mouths drop open simultaneously and immediately a crowd gathers round me in the changing room to gawp at my multi-coloured shin.

I have to admit it is pretty impressive, though no one had noticed until now because it was hidden beneath my trousers. But now I've taken them off for PE it's on display for everyone to see. I should have remembered that for drama queens like the Barbies a simple zit is a cause for hysteria, let alone a massive bruise like this.

'What did you do?' asks Lissa.

'Fell over.'

'When?'

'Saturday.' Immediately I wish I could take

back that one little word and change it to Sunday as I watch her face cloud over.

'At your gran's?' she says suspiciously.

'Yep, at my gran's,' I say with a sigh.

'How come?'

'She lives on a hill. I took a tumble.'

'Like Jack and Jill!' giggles Georgia and her clones join in. I silence them with a look. I knew this would happen. A mass inquisition. I should've been better prepared.

'Have you broken it?' asks Tash.

'No, of course I haven't broken it,' I say scathingly, though I must admit exactly that thought had crossed my mind when Marvyn's boot had come into collision with my shin. The pain had taken my breath away and brought tears to my eyes. I'd dashed them away quickly before he could see them. They're such a girly thing, tears.

'Does it hurt?' asks Ali, stretching out her hand to touch it, and automatically I jerk it away. Ouch!

'Not if you leave it alone!' I say between gritted teeth.

'What's going on?' comes a voice and Mrs Waters, our PE teacher, makes an entrance.

'Look at Dani's leg, Miss!' shrieks Zadie. *Oh no!*

'It's nothing!' I say, but the teacher's eyes widen and she kneels down to examine it.

'That's quite an injury. Have you had this seen to?'

'Yes, Miss,' I say. 'My mum's a nurse.'

It's only half a lie. Mum is a nurse. But she hasn't seen it. I don't want her to. Too many questions. I pull my sock up over my shin and busy myself lacing up my hockey boots.

'What happened?'

'She fell over,' says Zadie importantly, loving the drama.

'Really?' Mrs Waters raises her eyebrows. 'It looks more like a contact injury to me. Does your mum say you're OK to play hockey on it, Dani?'

'Yes, Miss.'

'Good. Because you could earn a place at the Junior Development Centre if you continue to play as well as you have been. I'm considering putting you forward for it.'

Everyone cheers and I can feel myself beaming. I'm not quite sure how it works but I know that basically it means you get extra training so you can play at county level. Sounds good to me.

'Are you considering putting anyone else forward, Miss?' asks Lissa hopefully.

'Not yet, Lissa,' says Mrs Waters. 'It's most unusual for a Year Seven student to get into the centre. I don't know if it's happened before. But Dani's exceptional.' Lissa's face falls. 'That doesn't mean you stop trying,' adds Mrs Waters kindly. 'You could be next. Now, come on, you lot, hurry up outside. We've got a lesson to get on with.'

The field is muddy and it's not easy practising our skills. My leg hurts. I'll be glad when the new all-weather pitch is in place that we raised money for before half term. We put on an eco fashion show, not my sort of thing at all, but it turned out to be an awesome evening. Ali masterminded it all with Lissa and Austen's help but she kept the finale a secret till the very last minute. She's a real dark horse that one, not even Lissa guessed what she was up to and it's hard to pull the wool over *her* eyes, I can tell you.

We move from skills to a game, then finally we troop off the field, covered in mud. Or in my case, hobble off. My leg has held up but it's really throbbing now.

Nothing wrong with my ears though. Mum always says I'm like a cat, my hearing is so good. Behind me Ali is brimming with sympathy. 'Poor old Dani, she looks like she's in agony.'

I'm about to turn round and say I'm all right when I hear someone mutter, 'She never got that bruise falling down.' It's Lissa. I ignore her and carry on walking, trying my best not to limp.

'What d'you mean?' Tash's voice chips in.

'You heard Mrs Waters,' Lissa says in a low voice. 'She said it looked like a contact injury, and she should know.'

'So?' Tash's voice is challenging. She knows Lissa's up to something but she doesn't know what.

I do. Lissa's no fool. Her next words confirm she's on to me.

'Dani said she couldn't meet up with us on Saturday cos she had to go to her gran's.'

'And your point is . . .?' says Tash, sounding bored.

'Duh! My point is she never went to her gran's

at all. She went and played football with her mates instead of coming out with us.'

Like I said. You can't pull the wool over Lissa's eyes.

Chapter 5

I hate people talking about me behind my back.
I turn round and stare Lissa straight in the eye.
'You got something to say to me, say it to my
face.'

The three of them stop short, shocked. It
doesn't sound like me, happy-go-lucky Dani –
normally so laidback I'm practically horizontal.

To Lissa's credit, even though her face is
scarlet, she sticks to her guns.

'I'm not having a go at you, Dani, but it's
pretty obvious you got that bruise playing football.'

'What if I did?'

'You said you'd come out with us on Saturday.'

'I know. I was going to. But I told you, I had
to see my gran instead.'

'Yeah, right. So how come you got that great

big bruise then? Kick you in the shins, did she?' She laughs like it's a joke but I know it's not.

They're all staring at me, waiting.

'Get a move on, you lot!' shouts Mrs Waters from the changing rooms. 'The bell's about to go!'

'Come on,' says Ali, her face troubled, and she breaks into a run. Lissa and Tash follow her, leaving me to bring up the rear. No one says anything while we're getting dressed. I deliberately take my time, seething with rage because I feel that Lissa has backed me into a corner. The others leave before me. When I finally emerge from the changing rooms break is over and it's time for the next lesson.

The house is quiet when I get home from school that day. My mum's a nurse practitioner at a GP surgery in town and on the days that she works late Jade goes to after-school clubs till Mum's ready to collect her. Since I started at Riverside I'm allowed to come straight home. I'm not on my own for long and I quite like it. I usually change out of my uniform and get my homework done and out of the way. Or sometimes I go and kick a ball around with the lads in the street till the others come home and tea's ready.

Today I don't know what I want to do. I'm feeling all churned-up inside.

Nobody had said any more to me about playing football, not even Lissa. If they had, maybe I would've told them the truth. Nobody had another go at me, but all day it was awkward. After French it was lunchtime and we went and sat at our usual picnic bench. The atmosphere was strained and for the first time since we'd got to know each other it was like nobody could think of anything to say.

But then Lissa, who loves her food, started talking about the panini she'd had on Saturday and then Tash went into raptures about what she'd had to eat. It turned out they'd sat chatting in the cafe for so long they'd ended up having lunch there as well. Then they started telling me about how the Barbies had seen them and they'd come into the cafe and ordered something to eat too, making out this was what they did all the time, but Chantelle couldn't even pronounce what she was asking for. And they all seemed to think this was hilarious but it didn't seem that funny to me. It just seemed

artificial, like everyone was pretending everything was normal when it wasn't.

Afterwards they'd gone round the shops and
tried stuff on. I'm really not interested in clothes
shopping and I thought Ali wasn't either, but
today she was as bad as the other two. I made
an effort to join in the conversation but it's hard
if you weren't there and, anyway, it was really
boring. In the end I just sat there grinning and
nodding and let them rabbit on. And on. And
on.

I found out something weird today.

You can be on your own and not feel lonely
at all. But you can be in the middle of your
best mates, looking like you're having the time
of your life, and inside you feel completely
isolated.

I take out my history work and start writing
up notes I'd made in the lesson. After that I try
to learn some French vocab but it's no good,
my heart's not in it. I pick up my phone and
find myself pressing Lissa's number. I need to
apologize to her for snapping her head off, for
my sake as much as hers. I hate atmospheres,
they freak me out. It reminds me what it was
like when Mum and Dad were breaking up.

But Lissa's number is busy. She's on the phone to someone. Tash or Ali, no doubt. I bet they're talking about me.

There's a knock on the door. A kid from down the street is standing there with a football under his arm.

'Wanna game?' he asks hopefully.

I hesitate. I really want to but my leg is sore and I've played a full game of hockey on it already today. It's important that it's completely healed by Saturday. I put my phone back to my ear. It's still engaged.

'Yeah,' I say, hanging up. 'Why not?'

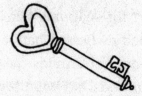

Chapter 6

By the time Mum and Jade walk down the street quite a few of us are out there having a kick-around, all of them lads except me, but I'm used to that. 'Tea in half an hour,' Mum calls as she puts her key in the lock.

It's starting to get dark when I go in and the light is on in the kitchen. My sister's already sitting at the table, chatting away to Mum who is serving up plates of pasta with Bolognese sauce. I slip into my place feeling loads better. It must be those endorphins Mrs Waters is always banging on about which flood your body after you've done some strenuous exercise. Happy hormones, she calls them, which Tash thinks is hilarious. Or maybe it's simply the sight and smell of food.

Mum places a hot, steaming plate of pasta

in front of Jade and me then sits down with hers beside us. Across from her, Dad's chair sits empty, a constant reminder of his absence from our family, like a gap where a painful tooth has been extracted.

They're all around the house these gaps: a bare display cabinet where his football trophies used to stand; a drying rack full of dainty underwear, but devoid of boxer shorts or novelty socks; no shaving foam or razor or unused bottle of Christmas aftershave on the bathroom shelf; three toothbrushes in the cup, not four.

I start to feel miserable again.

Mum sighs as if she's reading my mind, or perhaps she's just tired from being at work all day. 'What's all this about you hurting your leg?' she asks and forks food into her mouth.

News travels fast when you've got a mum like mine. The bush telegraph, the jungle drums, Twitter, none of them can compete with her. Information runs through her faster than the speed of light – she doesn't just follow me, she knows what's happening in my life before I do.

At least, she thinks she does.

'Knocked it playing football.' I'm aware of it aching now I've been running about on it again, but I add quickly, 'It's no big deal. How did you find out?'

'Tash was at the surgery with her mum and the boys. When did you do it?' She sounds only mildly interested. The advantage of having a mum who's a nurse is that she's seen every injury and disease under the sun and you have to be on your deathbed before she's the least bit impressed.

'Saturday.'

She frowns at me, puzzled, and I explain. 'I had a knock-about with some kids in the park by Gran's house. Got a bit of a bump, that's all.'

She shakes her head. 'What are you like? I thought Riverside Academy might have made a lady of you at last. Especially when you did that fashion show. But here you are, still chasing a football around.'

'A lady?' I snort derisively. 'It was ace. I really enjoyed it. I'm going to play with them again this Saturday.'

Jade rolls her eyes and Mum laughs. 'Football mad she is, just like her dad,' she says, but her voice sounds a bit wistful. I hesitate, wondering how much to tell her, but then she turns to Jade and asks her about school and the moment passes.

It all began last half term, way before the fashion show, when Jade and I went over to Gran's on our own for the first time. Since I started at Riverside Mum's been giving me more rein, letting me go places under my own steam, encouraging me to meet up with my new friends. The only proviso is if she's working on Saturdays I have to have Jade with me. I'm not stupid, she's using me as an unpaid babysitter!

I don't mind; Jade's no trouble. The first thing we did was go over to see Gran on the train on our own and that set the pattern for Saturdays ever since, whether Mum's working or not.

It's not just that I like Gran's company, which I do. Not as much as Jade does though. Those two are like a pair of kids when they get together. They love going round charity shops, poking through piles of unwanted items to find steals in vintage clothing, bric-a-brac, books . . . Of course books.

I got bored rigid that first Saturday and after a while wandered off down the park and let them get on with it. Some boys were having a knock-around on the football pitch so I stopped to watch them. One of them hit the ball into the bushes next to me so I retrieved it and lobbed it back to him.

'Thanks!' he called. He had bright ginger hair and looked nice. A bit later the ball came my way again and I did a big drop kick back to him. He picked it up and this time he said, 'Wanna game? We're one short.'

I was really surprised to be asked. Don't get me wrong, I'll play football every chance I get but since I left primary school I've only played in the street with the kids I grew up with. Like, most boys don't want a girl in their team, plus these guys were pretty good. But I didn't need to be asked twice.

'All right.'

'Five-a-side. You're on my team. You, me, Vikram, Lofty and Marvyn. Against the others.'

I ran over to them and he passed the ball to me. I trapped it and flicked it from my toe to my knee and back for a few seconds while I worked out who was who. A boy tried to tackle me so I turned away and deflected it to a long gangly guy who I was pretty sure must be Lofty.

He sent it straight back to me so I must've been right. I passed it on to the ginger kid who sliced it high and wide, but I raced down the pitch overtaking the rest of them and picked up the ball and lobbed it into the net.

'Yay!' said the boy, high-fiving me. 'Nice work! My name's Ryan. What's yours?'

'Dani.'

'Welcome to the team, Danny,' he said and turned to the others. 'I think we've found our new man.'

Chapter 7

I never meant to mislead them. I never set out to pretend I was a boy.

I didn't even realize at that point that they actually didn't know I was a girl. When Ryan said, 'We've found our new man,' I thought he was being funny and I laughed, pleased they'd accepted me, and then we carried on playing. I played well, I know I did, my confidence boosted by the goodwill I could feel flooding towards me. It fired me up and made me rise to the occasion. I'd missed this standard of play. I was in my element.

Afterwards they crowded round me, wanting to know who I played for.

'Well, I was playing for Pengrowse but I've left now,' I explained, Pengrowse being my primary school.

'Come and play for us then!' said Ryan. 'We're getting a junior team together. My Uncle Terry says he'll train us up and he used to play for the Wanderers. How old are you?'

'Eleven.'

'Perfect.'

I couldn't believe my ears.

'Are you serious?' I knew that technically girls were allowed to play in boys' teams nowadays, but I didn't know a single girl who'd ever been asked to play in one. Not at this level anyway.

They all started nodding their heads and saying, 'Yeah, yeah!' and 'You bet!' and stuff like that, and I found myself grinning with delight. But then Lofty said, 'We need lads like you.'

'What d'you mean?' I asked, my smile fading.

'Lads who are first-class players,' he said simply. 'Like you.'

Oh no! The penny dropped. He thought I was a boy. I looked around at all the faces waiting eagerly for my decision. They all did! They all thought I was a boy!

Why was I so surprised? Everyone thinks I'm a boy when I first meet them. Even Lissa said, 'I didn't know boys were allowed in this school,' when we started at Riverside. I look like one, let's face it, with my short spiky hair and freckles and my stocky build. I don't mind, it doesn't bother me!

I wish I had been a boy. They have loads more fun.

But now I had the opportunity to have some fun too. To play the game I loved every week to a respectable standard with a bunch of guys who were passionate about it. It was my dream come true.

Now was the time to come clean and fess up that actually I was a girl and see if they still wanted me.

But I hesitated. What if they didn't? This was the best chance I'd ever had to play football at a decent level. I couldn't take the risk of losing it.

'OK then!' I said and a cheer went up as they all piled on top of me.

What have I done? Now I'm committed to playing every single week with these guys and very soon we're going to have our first actual match against another side. I can't leave them in the lurch now, it's too late for that.

I don't want to anyway, I'm loving it.

I'm in this to the end.

Chapter 8

Football is my *raison d'être* (my 'reason for being' – we do French at Riverside, Madame Dupré would be proud of me) but until I started playing with the Blackett boys it was actually, to my huge regret, starting to disappear from my life. It was different when Dad was home. We used to eat, drink and sleep it then. Nearly every day when he came home from work we'd kick a ball around together. He taught me everything I know about the game. We'd watch it every opportunity we had on TV and he was forever reading me match reports out of the newspaper. Best of all, like I said before, we used to follow the Wanderers together.

I can't go and watch them any more because there's no one to take me and Mum won't let me go on my own.

It's not fair. Parents should think about these things before they split up.

Now school takes precedence over everything else. Mum was so proud when I won a scholarship to Riverside Academy, she went round telling everyone who would listen. I felt sorry for her poor patients because you could bet your life while she was dressing their wounds and sticking needles into them she was going on and on about my scholarship. I didn't even want to go to Riverside but there was no way she or Gran were ever going to let me turn it down.

I have to say though, she was right; it is a really good school, even if it doesn't take boys. I'm glad I came. Most of the time. I like playing hockey and netball (though not so much as football) and being captain of the hockey team and I'm glad that my PE teacher has spotted my potential. I like most of my subjects, in fact, and nearly all of my teachers.

But what I like best is being friends with Lissa, Ali and Tash.

I'd never had a close friend before. I just muddled along with everyone at primary school, spending most of my time in the playground with the boys. But now I've got not one, not two, but THREE best mates and, actually, that makes me feel special. We got to know each other sooooo quickly. I like them all equally but in different ways.

Girls are different from boys. They talk more together and do less. Girls like to tell their friends everything about themselves. We all promised we wouldn't keep anything from each other. Then we found out that both Ali and Tash had secrets.

Now it's my turn.

The good thing is none of us bears grudges. Nobody blamed Ali for not telling us about her sister and we could all see why Tash kept her home life hidden. Now I'm hoping Lissa won't still be cross with me for snapping at her yesterday. I know I was out of order and I can't help worrying that it will be a bit awkward between us still.

But when I go into my form room this morning and see my friends already there perched on the desks chatting, Lissa grins at me straight away, budging up so I can sit next to her.

'Wanna sweet?' she asks indistinctly, popping

another one in her mouth as she holds out a paper bag to me. She's always eating, mostly rubbish, even though her mum's a health freak apparently.

I shake my head and say, 'Sorry I had a go at you yesterday, Liss.'

She looks blank for a second like she's forgotten all about it and then puts her arm round my shoulders and gives me a hug.

'That's all right, babe, we all have our off days. I do definitely.'

Ali raises her eyebrows. 'You can say that again.'

'I do definitely,' repeats Lissa and we all giggle.

'We've got geography first,' remarks Tash and now we all groan, even Ali. Geography should be Ali's favourite lesson because she's into the environment in a big way but geography means Mr Little. I'm not kidding, that's really his name. What makes it even funnier is he's not little, he's extremely tall and thin with long bony wrists that poke out of the sleeves of his cord jacket, the same grubby jacket he wears every single day of his life. It's like somebody's told him that's the uniform geography teachers have to wear.

I don't mind that, I mean you don't expect teachers to be supermodels. He's younger and better looking than Grumpy Griffiths, our maths teacher, who's got grey beetley eyebrows and a warty nose. (Actually, the whole world is better looking than Grumpy Griffiths.) The difference is that Grumpy Griffiths, despite his name and his appearance, is a good teacher, while Mr Little is rubbish.

He doesn't know enough about his subject: he's not a geography specialist, he admitted that to us straight away which was probably a mistake. He was brought in on supply after half term when Mrs Jones went off on maternity leave. They should've asked Ali to teach us instead, she knows much more than he does. Or Lissa. She could control us better.

Mr Little just goes through the textbook every lesson and it's dead boring. Because it's boring, people start playing up and it always dissolves into chaos. You'd think it would be fun for the class if a teacher can't keep control but it's not, you get fed up with it after a while. The Barbies run rings around him. Today is no different.

'Open your books at Population,' says Mr Little and immediately people start clamouring.

'Where's my book?'

'Haven't got one, Sir!'

'What page?'

'What did he say?'

Mr Little clears his throat and tries again. 'Page forty-five. Now pay attention everyone. Chantelle, share your book with Georgia. Chantelle! I said share . . . Hmm. Now then. Danielle? Can you read please?'

I hate being called Danielle.

'The population of the British Isles rose signif-icantly after the Industrial Revolution,' I begin.

Zadie (in a whisper just loud enough for everyone to hear): 'That's because they were all at it like rabbits.' We start giggling and Mr Little's face turns pink.

Georgia: 'I reckon England should have a one-child policy.'

Ali (considering the concept, which she finds genuinely interesting): 'Like China, you mean?'

Zadie: 'What about Scotland? If England has one, Scotland should too.'

Chantelle: 'And Wales.'

Georgia: 'Mrs Jones was from Wales. Has Wales got a one-child policy, Sir?'

Mr Little: 'Um, no. No, it doesn't.'

Georgia (with a sly grin): 'Didn't think so.' Zadie and Chantelle giggle but no one else does. Most of us were big fans of Mrs Jones, our last geography teacher, who'd gone off to have her third baby.

'You're not clever, Georgia,' says Lissa, sounding bored.

Georgia (looking annoyed, but refusing to let it go): 'Sir, d'you think we should have a one-child policy?'

Mr Little (thinking he's finally caught her interest at last): 'Well, yes, it's certainly an interesting question, Georgia. If you consider that the population has doubled since –'

Georgia: 'So are you telling us we should use birth control, Sir?'

Mr Little (realizing too late it's a trap, and flushing fiery red): 'Um, I'm not sure we should be discussing this . . .'

'You're not being funny, Georgia, you're just being rude!' says Lissa loudly and sternly. Georgia turns round with a wounded look on her face.

'No, I'm not, I'm just asking questions,' she says pretending to be hurt. 'If I was being rude

I would be saying things like, *Sir, your lessons are boring* or *Sir, your coat sleeves are too short.* Or *Sir . . .*'

'Georgia, shut up!' says Lissa, her voice full of command, and Georgia does as she's told.

You don't want to mess with Lissa. I'm glad she's my friend, not my enemy. I carry on reading aloud to the now silent class. The door opens and the headmistress pokes her head round.

'Everything all right, Mr Little?' she asks and he nods nervously.

'Everything's fine, thank you, Mrs Shepherd.'

But I can't help noticing how he darts a grateful glance towards Lissa as the head closes the door.

Chapter 9

This Saturday it turns out that Tash is doing something with her family and only Lissa and Ali have plans to meet up. Maybe because of this there seems to be less pressure on me to join them.

'You going to see your gran again this weekend, Dani?' asks Lissa and I nod.

'Yep, we're all going. Mum too.'

'I think it's lovely the way you visit your grandmother every week,' says Ali. 'I watched a programme on the telly last night and it was all about how lonely old people are nowadays. It's because they're stuck inside all day with nothing to do and nobody ever goes to see them.'

I think of my jet-propelled gran whizzing

around between home and gym and school, and theatre and tennis club and golf course, and lunching and swimming and shopping, and wonder if she actually minds us turning up each week to disturb her busy life. I'm such a fake. People think I'm being kind and unselfish when actually I'm not. I'm even fooling my own mother. Last night she asked Jade and me what our plans were for Saturday.

Jade looked at me and I said, 'Gran's?' and she nodded happily. Easy-peasy.

'You don't have to,' said Mum. 'I'm not working this weekend. We could do something else if you want.'

'Can we go swimming?' Jade asked eagerly.

'If you want to,' Mum said. 'Do you want to come, Dani? Or maybe you'd like to meet up with your friends instead?'

I stared at them both in alarm. No way! This Saturday would be our last but one chance to train together. In two weeks' time we were going to play our first match as Blackett Juniors.

'Jade! Gran will be expecting us. We don't want to disappoint her.'

Jade looked a bit shamefaced but Mum

smiled at me. 'That's really sweet of you, Dani,' she said. 'Maybe I should come too.'

It was my turn to feel ashamed. Then immediately I started worrying that if Mum came with us to see Gran she might find out what I'm really up to.

Now Ali's making me feel bad as well. I'm a fraud. Everyone thinks I'm being really kind to my poor old granny, going all that way to visit her each week. Whereas I know my motives are not quite so pure. I love my gran but the simple reason I make that trip to Blackett each Saturday without fail is so that I can play with Ryan and the others. It's the best opportunity I've ever had to play class football and I'm not going to blow it.

Gran, though she doesn't know it, is my alibi.

Lissa's eyes flick towards my leg. The bruise has all but disappeared now, just a faint blue and yellow shadow left to remind me where Marvyn's size eights collided with my shin last week. It strikes me that Lissa is the only person who's not completely taken in by my Little Red Riding Hood act. Maybe it's because, like me, she doesn't believe in fairy tales.

'Actually,' I concede, seeing the lack of conviction in her eyes, 'I'm hoping to have a knockabout while I'm there.'

'I knew it!' she says triumphantly. 'I knew you'd played football last Saturday.'

'Yeah, I did. But that's not the reason I couldn't meet up with you,' I add quickly. 'Only sometimes, when I'm at my gran's, it gets a bit boring so I wander down the park and see if there's anyone I can have a quick game with.'

'Why didn't you say that before?'

'Because you made out I was lying and I was mad at you!' I say aloud.

Because you made out I was lying and I was, I say inside my head.

'Sorry!' She manages to look contrite for one second flat, then grins. 'Come on then, tell us! Who kicked you in the shin?'

'A guy called Marvyn. He's only my age but he wears size eights.'

'I know a boy called Marvyn,' says Tash thoughtfully. 'He's brilliant at football. I wonder if it's the same guy?'

My heart plummets.

'What's his surname?'

I shrug. 'Dunno. I don't know him that well.'

'Find out if it's Marvyn Bailey. I bet it's him.'

'Bailey!' Lissa's eyes light up. 'That's Ajay's surname.'

We all groan. Lissa was mad about Ajay, a boy who lives on Tash's estate, till she found out he was only interested in Tash. She still fancies him though, it's obvious.

Lissa is really getting into boys, not like the rest of us. Well, I'm into boys but only because I wish I *was* a boy. And, as far as I know, Ajay and Tash are just good friends, like Ali and her mate, Austen.

'He's Ajay's cousin,' explains Tash.

'Ooh! Maybe we should come and watch you play, Dan,' says Lissa. 'If this Marvyn is anything like Ajay –'

'He isn't,' I say shortly, nipping this idea in the bud. 'You don't even know if he *is* Ajay's cousin.'

'Find out for me, will you?' she asks, going all girly and giggly.

Aargh! She can be sooooo annoying.

Ever wish you'd kept your mouth shut?

Chapter 10

When Gran opens her front door and sees Mum her face breaks into a huge smile.

'Pam, darling!' she says and envelops her in a massive hug.

Mum and Gran don't see too much of each other nowadays.

By the time Dad officially left us, Jade and I were sort of used to him not being around any more and I didn't really appreciate that he was never going to come back and live with us again. Mum kind of protected us from all that.

She got a new job at the surgery and threw herself into full-time work, enrolling my sister and me in breakfast and after-school clubs. We just got on with it. When Mum and Dad got divorced we hardly noticed. But then this summer holidays, just before I started at Riverside Academy, he quietly got married again. He didn't even invite Jade or me to the wedding. I think Mum was cross about that because I heard her having a go at him. He said it was better that way, he didn't want to upset us.

He did though.

Now we don't see much of him and increasingly we don't really talk much about him either. It doesn't mean I miss him any the less though. Sometimes I just wish I could have a really good conversation about the break-up and divorce with Mum or Dad and why it happened and clear the air once and for all.

The trouble is when Dad does come back to see us he's desperate to know that Jade and I are happy. It's so obvious he feels guilty about leaving us; I can't add to it by bringing up the whys and wherefores of what he did. And it's sort of the same with Mum. I constantly feel that I need to reassure them both that, OK, they're divorced and we hardly see my dad and he's married again and he's got two stepsons who I've never met, but so what? That's nothing out of the ordinary nowadays and I'm fine with it.

Only, the truth is, I'm not. I want my dad back.

Anyway, like I said, Mum doesn't see much of Gran any more. Which is good for me in one way because it means the two of them aren't constantly checking up on me. But it's bad too, because it's pretty obvious they really like each other.

Today they are yacking away together like nobody's business over cups of filter coffee, catching up on all the news. I hang about for a bit wondering when it will be safe for me to slip away. But just as I'm sidling out of the door Mum, who has eyes in the back of her head, says, 'Where do you think you're going?'

'Thought I'd just pop out for a bit.'

Mum stares at me. 'Where to?'

'Just out. The park. Wherever.'

She checks her watch. 'Before lunch?'

'I'm not hungry.'

'She gets bored hanging round here all day with nothing to do, don't you, Dani, love?' says Gran.

'Take Jade with you then,' says Mum, but I

answer quickly, 'She's reading. You don't want to come, do you, Jade?' and my sister, on the sofa where's she's stretched out with a book, predictably shakes her head.

'See you later,' I say and I'm out of the door and away down the hill before my mum can object further. I resist the temptation to check my appearance in the ladies' loos; no need any more, I must look sufficiently boyish because I've got away with masquerading as one for long enough. As I enter the park I can see most of the lads already assembled on the big patch of grass between the trees and my heart beats faster. There's about fourteen of us now. I can't wait to play.

Today Ryan's Uncle Terry is watching us carefully. He's been brilliant, helping us to register the team for the league and coaching us each week. He used to play for West Park Wanderers and he's really good. At the end of play today he's going to select the team for our first proper game as Blackett Juniors in two weeks' time.

He divides us into two teams and we get straight in. A pass from Lofty gives me possession of the ball and though Ryan bears down on me I outwit first him, then Nathan. A flick to Vikram and he takes a shot at goal (two hoodies, required distance apart) only to be foiled by Sean who flings his body across to save it. We don't let up though and by half-time it's three–nil and I've scored two of them. Terry gives me the thumbs-up. This is ace.

I'm getting my breath back and enjoying a swig of water from Ryan's bottle when suddenly I freeze. Strolling along the path, not twenty metres away from me, are my mum and Gran, with my sister trailing behind them. They walk straight past us, deep in conversation, but Jade looks up and our eyes meet. She comes to a stop and opens her mouth to say something. I put my finger to my lips and shake my head, my eyes pleading. She darts a look at Mum and Gran and back to me and nods, then hurries on after them.

'Who's that?' asks Ryan who's witnessed it all.

'My sister.'

'What's with all the secrecy?'

'I'm not supposed to be playing football,'

I say shortly. 'I didn't want her to tell my mum.'

'Why not?'

'Don't ask,' I mutter and wander away from his questions till we're ready to start the second half. Terry swaps in some people who didn't get a game in the first half but I get to stay on. I wish I hadn't, I'm rubbish. I'm shaken to the core by the close shave I've just had and my concentration is shot to pieces as I keep an eye out for Mum and Gran in case they walk back. There's no sign of them though and in the end we scrape a win, four–three, no thanks to me.

'Right then, lads, over here,' calls Terry, and everyone runs to him obediently, eager to find out if they've made the team. I know I haven't. I've blown it by my performance in the second half. Terry's next words confirm my fears.

'What happened to you, Danny?'

'Dunno,' I say glumly. 'Think I just got tired.'

'Hmm.' Terry shakes his head and Ryan looks as disappointed as I do.

Maybe it was for the best. I was never going to be able to keep up this charade for long. I just hope I don't cry when my name is left off the list.

But it's not. To my huge surprise Terry reads my name out and I'm so thrilled I want to scream or hug someone or do a crazy dance.

But of course I don't, because that would kind of give the game away, wouldn't it?

Chapter 11

On Monday morning Lissa strolls into class, digs her hand into her bag and pulls out a pile of pale pink envelopes.

'One for you, one for you, one for you . . .' she says, doling them out to Ali, Tash and me.

'What is it?'

'Open it and see.'

Tash tears open the envelope and pulls out a pretty pink card with a cupcake on it. 'PARTY!' she squeals in delight. Lots of heads turn our way including the Barbies'.

'Is it your birthday, Liss?' asks Chantelle sweetly.

'Certainly is,' says Lissa. 'I'll be twelve. I'm ancient compared to most of you lot.'

'You're ancient compared to me. I'm not

twelve till next July,' I agree and examine the card. 'Trust you to have a cake on the front.'

'Mine's next month,' says Georgia. 'I'm having a party too. You're invited, Lissa.'

Lissa ignores her and waves an invite in front of Tori's nose. 'Wanna come?'

'Yes please!'

'When is it?' asks Zadie, but Lissa doesn't appear to hear her.

'Here's yours, Ella.'

'Thanks!'

'And yours, Nisha.'

'Thanks, Lissa!'

'And one for you two.' She drops an invite on the table in front of the two clones, Chloe and Emma (known as Chlemma because they're always together).

'Thank you!' they chorus.

'When did you say your birthday was?' repeats Georgia.

'A week Saturday.'

My heart misses a beat. 'A week Saturday?'

'Yep. But the party's this Friday evening. It fits in better for my mum.'

Phew! 'Cool,' I say. 'Can't wait.'

'Dress code optional,' she adds. 'Or in your case, trouser code.'

'Ha ha!' I pull my funny face at her, the one where I cross my eyes and stick my tongue out of the side of my mouth and she pulls it back at me.

'By the way,' she says to Ali. 'It's OK to bring Austen along.'

'Really?' says Ali, looking surprised but pleased. 'OK, I'll ask him.'

'And bring Ajay too if you want, Tash,' she says, like it's an afterthought.

I roll my eyes.

'What?' she says.

'You are soooo obvious.' I can't believe she's still carrying a torch for Ajay.

'He's Tash's boyfriend, not mine!' she says, laughing.

'He's not my boyfriend!' says Tash automatically.

'That's all right then, he's up for grabs!' retorts Lissa. Then, as she sees the look of alarm on Tash's face, she adds kindly, 'I'm only teasing. We all know he's crazy about you. Tell him to bring a good-looking mate for me instead.

Here, give him an invite. There's plenty more where these came from.'

Georgia sidles up to her. 'So, um, Lissa? What time did you say the party started?' Behind her, Chantelle and Zadie smile at us ingratiatingly.

Lissa turns to face them. 'I didn't.' She makes a deliberate show of tucking the remaining envelopes away in her bag. 'Sorry, girls, I've run out of invites.'

Georgia looks furious, while Zadie and Chantelle immediately start squawking things like 'Cheek!' and 'I never wanted to go anyway!' and 'Who wants to go to her house? She's a snob!' They sound like a pair of demented chickens and I can't help laughing out loud. It's pretty mean of Lissa but they deserve it. The Barbies are trouble-makers, all three of them, and full of gossip. Like the rumour they spread about Tash's mum. They get away with it because everyone's afraid of getting on the wrong side of them.

Except for Lissa. She's not afraid of them. Good old Lissa.

'What are you laughing at?' Georgia snaps at me suddenly.

'Nothing!' I say and she flounces off. Typical!

Lissa's rattled her cage but it's me she's having a go at.

So? I'm not scared of Georgia and her cronies either. It was me that called them the Barbies in the first place because they're empty-headed dolls that all look the same. They can't do anything to me.

The Barbies are the least of my worries.

Chapter 12

I am going to be super-fit!

Either that or I'm training myself into an early grave! It's not just football training on Saturdays, it's hockey practice at school. Every day!

Mrs Waters has had me out on that mucky field practising skills all this week, both lunch-times and after school. Can't wait for the all-weather pitch! It couldn't have been worse weather and the ground is really soggy, but she won't let up. She's determined to see if I'm up to the standard for Junior Development training.

Tash says I'm Mrs Water's *protégée*. It's a French word (another one – move over, Madame Dupré!), meaning I'm her special discovery who she wants to make as good as her or even better. Tash's vocabulary is amazing. I hope I do get to be as good as my teacher at hockey one day.

It's a great game, though not as good as football of course.

Lissa and Tash and Ali have turned out with me too. Tash can't make every after-school practice because sometimes she has to pick up her little brother Keneil from nursery but she comes when she can and she makes all the lunchtime sessions. Ali comes to everything, even though she's not even in the Year Seven team, and so does Lissa. I think Lissa's still hoping that Mrs Waters will put her in for training too.

Georgia doesn't come at all, even though she is in the team.

'She's a good player but if it's not about her she doesn't want to know,' remarks Lissa as we shower and change at the end of after-school practice on Thursday. Actually, that's what I used to think Lissa was like but she isn't when you get to know her, she's just competitive.

'You can't be like that if you're a member of a team, you've got to pull your weight,' I say, rubbing my hair dry.

'I reckon she's still sulking because Lissa didn't invite her to her party,' says Tash. 'Oohh, I can't wait for tomorrow!'

Tomorrow night, Ali, Tash and I are going straight to Lissa's after school and getting ready there. I can't wait to see Lissa's house; Ali's the only one of us who's been there and she says it's awesome.

'I still don't know what to wear,' says Tash and we all groan. She changes her mind every day. 'No, really,' she protests, 'I can't choose between my little white lace dress which I wear absolutely everywhere –'

'I've never even seen you in a little white lace dress,' I say, but she ignores me.

'– or my skinniest jeans with a vest top and fur waistcoat combo –'

'Fur!' shrieks Ali. 'You can't wear fur!'

'It's not real fur!'

'That's not the point. So long as you wear it, whether it's fake or not, you're signalling to people that it's OK to kill animals for their pelts –'

'For their what?' interrupts Lissa.

'Their pelts. Their coats. The only creature that should wear a leopard-skin coat is a leopard.'

'It's not leopard skin.'

'What is it then?'

66

'I don't know, it's just fur.'

'See? You don't even care enough to know what animal has been killed to make your waistcoat.'

'Aargh! No animal *has* been killed, it's fake!'

The two best friends glare at each other: quiet, gentle Ali, whose alter ego is fierce environmental campaigner, and Tash, who, beneath her superficial, fun-loving exterior is actually kind and thoughtful.

'OK,' concedes Tash, 'I'll wear my little white lace dress *again*,' and Ali flings her arms round her.

'I LOVE that little white lace dress.'

Lissa rolls her eyes. 'That's decided then. Now, what are you wearing, Dani?'

But she doesn't wait for a reply because she's joking. Everyone knows I'm not into fashion.

I'll just be tomboy Dani in my jeans and T-shirt.

Chapter 13

Friday lunchtime, before we go to Lissa's, we do another hockey practice. With the bad weather we've had all week, the ground is like a bog. By the time our PE teacher has finished with us we're soaked through and filthy dirty. I can't tell you how many times we slip and fall on our backsides in the mud but she won't let up till the bell goes for afternoon school. Sadist!

There's no time to shower so when we change we get mud all over our uniforms. All afternoon we have to sit in lessons listening to the Barbies making witty comments (not!) like: 'Pooh!' 'It stinks in here!' 'It's like a pig-sty,' 'Who let the dogs out?' and the slightly more droll 'Good body hygiene is soooo important, don't you think?' from Georgia who always smells like the perfume counter at Boots.

68

So I say, 'Didn't you know, Georgia? Mud is good for the complexion; you should try it,' which is a bit mean because she just happens to have a rather prominent zit on her nose. It raises a laugh and makes up for us having to sit there all afternoon, mucky, damp and cold.

'Never mind,' says Lissa when we finally get out of school. 'You can all have a nice bath or shower when you get to my house,' and we cheer up.

From outside Lissa's house looks tall and posh. Like her. It's one of those Georgian houses that has a little front garden with pots of miniature ornamental trees and spiked railings. The windows are divided into small panes and the front door is black and solid with a shiny brass knocker and you know that absolutely no one would ever be allowed through it except by invitation only.

The door swings open and Mrs Hamilton is standing there. She must've been waiting for us.

'Come in! Come in!' she says, and even though she's smiling it's more like an order than an invitation. We shuffle in obediently, taking our shoes off in the hallway like Lissa does.

Inside it's A-MAZ-ING! Ali had said it was like a house in a magazine, the ones you get in the doctor's surgery, and it really is. It's all carpets and soft lights and expensive furniture. There are floor-to-ceiling bookcases and a piano and soft sofas and a huge table in the dining room with matching chairs, and flowers everywhere. Everything is immaculate.

Lissa's mum offers us drinks and there's a choice of fresh juices or a variety of teas, most I've never heard of, or filter coffee with cream and sugar, or hot chocolate with cream and marshmallows. We all plump for the hot chocolate.

'Are you sure?' she says, looking at Lissa. 'Wouldn't you prefer some juice, darling?'

'No!' says Lissa. 'I said chocolate, didn't I?' which is a bit rude I think. Her mum serves it in a kitchen that's like one you see advertised on TV. I wish my mum could see it. We all sit at a big unit in the centre which Mrs Hamilton calls 'the island', on high stools with little backs to them, and sip our hot chocolate out of tall glasses, fishing the marshmallows out with long spoons. And you know what? It's made of real chocolate, not powder, no wonder it tastes so delicious! And there's a big plate of crunchy oat biscuits with chocolate chunks to go with them, and they're delicious too.

I wish Mrs Hamilton was my mum. (Only joking, Mum!)

But when Lissa helps herself to a second biscuit, Mrs Hamilton says, 'That's enough, Melissa,' and whisks the plate away from her. My mum would never do that to me in front of my friends. Lissa goes bright pink but she doesn't say anything. Mrs Hamilton offers the plate to the rest of us but now no one wants to look greedy so we refuse politely and she takes it away, even though we're all dying for another one and there are loads left. It's dead awkward.

Actually, I'm glad Mrs Hamilton isn't my mum. I prefer my own.

'Would you like to clean up a bit and get ready for the party?' she asks, looking at my muddy nails. I hide them quickly in my lap. 'There's plenty of hot water.'

'Yes please. You go first,' I say to Ali, feeling a bit shy.

'No, you go first,' says Ali, obviously feeling a bit shy too.

'*I'll* go first!' says Tash who's never felt shy in her life.

'We can all go first,' says Lissa. 'No one needs to wait.'

When Lissa said we could all have a bath or a shower at her house I didn't realize she meant all at the same time! She's got not one, not two, not three, but FOUR bathrooms! There are only four people in her family: Lissa, her brother and her mum and dad. That's one each!

'Imagine having a bathroom to yourself,' squeals Tash as she dives into Lissa's en suite. 'You are soooooo lucky!'

'Bags me this one,' says Ali and disappears into what I think is the family bathroom.

'Whose is this?' I ask, peering into a bedroom. It's massive.

'My mum and dad's,' says Lissa and I shut the door quickly. 'I'll use that one. You can have my brother's if you want.'

Lissa's brother is captain of his rugby team at school and that's all I know about him.

'He's not going to walk in on me, is he?'

'No, of course not. He's gone to his mate's to avoid you lot and he's says he's not coming home till you've gone. Take your time.'

Mrs Hamilton appears carrying a big pile of neatly folded towels and hands me a couple. 'Here are some fresh towels for you, Danielle dear. I do hope Rupert has left everything tidy for you.'

Rupert! I'd forgotten Lissa's brother's name was Rupert. The only Rupert I've ever known apart from him is one that wears a red jumper, yellow check trousers and a matching scarf, and sits on Keneil's bed. Now I have a vision stuck in my head of Lissa's brother looking like Rupert Bear.

I sort of assume his room is going to be immaculate like the rest of the house but it's not, it's normal-boy messy. The curtains are still drawn but in the gloom I can make out an unmade bed, a computer with a dirty cereal bowl and mug next to it, and lots of discarded T-shirts and jeans and (avert my eyes!) boxer shorts on the floor. There's also a lingering warm sour boy smell.

Rupert may be posh but he's no different from any other boy. No yellow trousers or scarves or red jumpers. (Tee-hee!)

I skip quickly into the en suite which has towels on the floor and tubes of toothpaste and zit cream and other stuff left open. It feels weird being in some random boy's private space. It's not as if he was expecting anyone so it's all left out on display. There's probably really personal stuff here like . . . Don't go there, Dani. Take a deep breath.

I lock the door, slip off my clothes, play about with the shower control until it's the right temperature and step into the enclosure. Wow! It's a power shower and it's so strong! I stand underneath with steam rising round me, loving the sensation of hot water blasting my skin and no one rapping on the door telling me to get a move on. I'm never going to meet him (not tonight anyway), so I help myself to Rupert's shower gel, Rupert's body scrub and Rupert's shampoo and conditioner, and then, when I'm scalded and scrubbed to within an inch of my life, I turn off the shower, step out and wrap myself in the biggest, softest towel I have ever seen in my life.

I wind a smaller one round my hair in a turban, cover myself from face to toe in Rupert's moisturizer, pick up my uniform off the floor and stuff it into my bag. Then I pick my way daintily through the bedroom, taking particular

care to avoid the discarded boxers. I open the
bedroom door and peek out. No one about.

Carrying my bag full of clothes and wearing
nothing but a towel and bright pink skin, I go
in search of the others.

Chapter 14

They're in Lissa's room in various stages of undress.

'Look at you!' giggles Ali when she sees me wrapped in a towel. She's the most fully clothed of us all in her cotton leggings and print top. Tash is wandering around in her bra and pants (I didn't know she wore a bra!), still torn between the fur combo and the white lacy dress. Lissa is standing in jeans and bra (I knew she wore one), daubing some stuff on her face.

'What you wearing, Dani?' she asks.

In reply I unzip my bag and pull out my jeans and favourite T-shirt. Uh-oh! I shouldn't have stuffed my muddy school uniform on top of them.

'You can't wear those!' says Tash. I stare at them glumly. They're crumpled, damp and mucky. I give them a good shake and try to rub the mud off but it only makes them worse.

'You'll look like a grub,' says Liss. 'Borrow something of mine.' She flings open her wardrobe door to display the entire contents of Topshop. 'Help yourself!' she says. So I do.

But here's the problem. Lissa's about a foot taller than me, so all the jeans and trousers I try on are way too long for me. And it doesn't help if I roll them up because even though Lissa is quite skinny, the waist is too big for me and they fall down over my hips and I look like Charlie Chaplin.

'You'll have to wear a dress,' she says and I say, 'No way!' and luckily for me they're all too big as well.

'What are we going to do?' says Tash and then Ali says, 'Come on! We've improvised before. Remember the fashion show?' She opens Lissa's drawers and rifles through the contents. 'Here we are,' she says triumphantly, waving a top in the air. 'Perfect!'

And you know something? It really is. It's a sleeveless sky-blue button-up shirt made of soft silky material, but not too girly, so I don't object to trying it on. It feels lovely against my skin.

Ali stares at me critically then whisks a thin brown belt off a pair of Lissa's jeans and buckles it round my waist. She's got an eye for clothes, even though she hates the fashion industry; she gets it from her sister.

'What d'you think?' she asks me. I study myself in the mirror. The shirt looks like a dress now but I like it, even though I can't remember when I last wore one. It makes my legs look longer.

'She needs shoes,' says Lissa, 'but mine are all too big.'

'If I wear my fur combo and boots instead of my little white dress she can have these,' says Tash, flashing her open-toed high heels at me.

Ali opens her mouth to object to the fur, sees the others glaring at her, and gives up. 'OK then, I'll paint her toenails.'

'I'm not having my toenails painted!' I object, but she's not listening. She paints my toenails bright red and then she paints red, white and blue stripes on my fingernails which I have to admit makes them look very eye-catching and patriotic. Then Lissa wants to try her foundation and blusher on me and after that Tash does my eyes with her kohl pencil and triple-effect super-lash mascara.

'Try my new organic lip gloss,' says Ali, offering it to me. 'It's Nikki's.'

'Me! Me! Me! Me!' squeals Tash, who is besotted with Ali's sister, and grabs it first. I watch how she puts it on, then copy her. I never thought I'd be doing this. We grin at each other.

'You look pretty,' I say.

'So do you,' says Tash to my surprise. No one's ever said I looked pretty before. 'Now then, let's see what I can do with your hair.'

She picks up her hair bag and advances on me. I sit there for ages while she blasts my roots with a warm dryer, then teases and flicks my hair into shape with a multitude of brushes and combs. I always thought it would be a real pain to have your hair fussed with, but actually it feels nice and relaxing and I almost fall asleep. Finally, she spikes it with the gel she's just given Lissa for her birthday and stands back and looks at me with a critical eye. 'Right then,' she says, 'you're done. What d'you think?'

I stand up to examine myself in Lissa's full-length mirror and am so surprised I take a step backwards.

I can't believe it's me.

'You look lovely!' squeals Ali.

'You look fabulous!' says Lissa.

I don't say a word. I just study the stranger in the mirror.

I look way older than me and much, much cooler with my new funky hairstyle. My trademark freckles have disappeared beneath a smooth layer of foundation and pinky-peach blusher. Instead, it's my eyes that stand out; they look enormous, rimmed with kohl and fringed with long black lashes. (How does mascara do that, make your eyelashes grow?) My glossed lips look fuller than usual and the blue shirt/dress, clinched in at the waist by Lissa's belt, accentuates my figure. (I didn't even know I had one!) And, best of all, I look soooooo tall in my heels – as tall as Lissa.

And the nails! Don't forget the nails: they're the finishing touch. It's like they're saying, OK, everyone, so I know I'm stunning but, hey, I don't take myself too seriously!

'Wow! I like it!' I say to my surprise and then I put my hand on my hip and do a twirl. My friends cheer.

'You look so different, no one will know who

you are!' says Tash, so I do my cross-eyed tongue-hanging-out look to remind them who I really am and they all fall apart laughing.

But you know something? She's right. When people start turning up for the party they either take a second look at me and shriek, or walk straight past without even recognizing me. It is so funny!

You know what? I'm loving this party, I really am. It's very flattering when people keep coming up to you and telling you how gorgeous you look. (Though it does occur to me that means I must look pretty rubbish normally.)

Plus there's the food. Mrs Hamilton has gone to town and I have NEVER seen so much food in my life, all of it labelled so we know exactly what we're eating.

Where do I begin? There are:

- little one-pot entrées of curried prawns (*Entrées* is French for starters. I'm getting soooo good at French!)
- salsa and avocado, hummus, and cream-cheese dips with carrot sticks, broccoli and tortilla chips
- spicy chicken wings

- mini pizzas
- taco shells with guacamole, sour cream, cheese, tomatoes and lettuce
- bagels with salmon and cream cheese
- miniature burgers with onions, pickles, mustard, ketchup or barbecue sauce
- potato skins
- ham, chicken or veggie wraps with mayonnaise
- bowls of crispy things
- stacks of cupcakes
- jugs of iced watermelon and pineapple juice
- sparkling fruit cocktails

I think I'm in heaven. I make a bit of a pig of myself actually, trying things I've never eaten before, but then so does everyone else.

I thought Tash's mum's party was good when we had a pizza night and played football but this is something else. I feel really grown-up.

If this is what being a teenager is going to be like, bring it on!

Chapter 15

The party fills up rapidly. Lissa's dad comes home, puts his head round the door of the kitchen where we're all standing around eating, grabs a plate of food and disappears. At least, I'm assuming he was Lissa's dad. He could've been any random guy in a suit who had heard there was posh nosh going free!

Then Austen arrives. Austen Penberthy is Ali's best mate from primary school and we all know him from the fashion show which he helped Ali to organize. Austen (shaved head, glasses, nice face) is an eco-warrior and he's wearing a T-shirt which says 'Save the Earth' that he's tie-dyed himself. Immediately he corners Tash to engage her in a heated debate about the implications of wearing fur, but having made his point he moves on to chat to others. Unlike Lissa's dad he's completely unfazed at being the only boy in a room full of glammed-up eleven- and twelve-year-old girls.

He's not the only boy for long though. After a while I notice a couple more helping themselves to drinks.

'Who are they?' asks Tash, then her jaw drops open as one of them drapes his arm round Lissa's shoulders. 'OMG!'

Lissa is looking completely relaxed, like she's used to having tall, good-looking, *mature* guys giving her a cuddle. I'm not kidding, this particular guy must be fifteen or sixteen at least!

'Lissa's got a boyfriend!' Tash splutters. 'I don't believe it! She never said!'

I believe it. I've always thought Lissa was a dark horse. I don't get it though. I thought she was mad about Ajay, Tash's friend. Lissa's life is even more complicated than mine.

And there was me worrying myself silly about my little secret! It pales into insignificance compared to hers. I wouldn't want Ajay if I could have him!

I give myself a little shake. What am I on about? I don't even like boys! Not in that way.

But if I did like boys, I'd like him.

I can't stop staring at him. He's got thick dark hair and broad shoulders and a gorgeous smile. He's smiling at Lissa like he thinks she's the best thing since sliced bread. Then he glances up and sees me staring at him and he smiles at me too, before bending his head to whisper in Lissa's ear.

Oh no! I can feel myself blushing!

I never blush.

'They're coming over!' yelps Tash and the two of us immediately look the other way.

'Hi!' says Lissa as cool as a cucumber, with the two boys in tow.

'Oh, hi!' I trill, turning round and acting really surprised to see her here at her own party. She gives me a funny look and says, 'Let me introduce you. This is Duncan.' She indicates the other boy: fair hair, T-shirt, baggy trousers.

Nice. But nothing special.

What is wrong with me? I never judge boys on their appearance normally. It's like I've not just had a makeover, I've had a personality transplant as well.

To my surprise Duncan extends his hand, first to Tash, then to me. 'Pleased to meet you,' he says.

'Pleased to meet you,' we mumble, and then Lissa continues, 'And this is Rupert.'

'Rupert,' I repeat as Gorgeous-Smile-Boy takes my hand. 'Your . . .'

'Brother.' She completes my sentence. He's looking at me like he finds me really amusing.

Horrified, I drop his hand and say, 'I thought you weren't coming!' which is just about the daftest thing I could say, seeing as I've never met him before in my life. His smile widens.

'I didn't know you were expecting me.'

'I wasn't! I mean . . . Lissa said you weren't coming . . . I mean . . . oh flip, I used your shower to get ready, you see . . .'

He leans towards me and sniffs hard. I jump back but not quickly enough. 'Thought so,' he says. 'You used my shower gel too.'

My face grows so hot I think I'm about to implode. I'm really tempted to make a joke of it, which is the way I normally get myself out awkward situations. The words are there, ready, in my head. *OK, I come clean. Get it? I used your shampoo, your conditioner and your body scrub as well. And your moisturizer.* But instead I stand there speechless, glowing like a beacon.

'You've gone bright red,' observes Lissa

annoyingly which makes me go redder still. She should know better being as she's the biggest blusher of the four of us. 'What's wrong with you, Dani?'

Can't she understand how embarrassing this is? Obviously not. To be fair to her, she's probably never seen me react like this before. Dani Jarvis, tomboy of Year Seven, doesn't do embarrassment. As if to confirm my thoughts she adds, 'Dani's mad about football. You two should have a lot in common.'

'Really? Who d'you follow?'

'West Park Wanderers.'

'Me too.' I'm treated to the full Gorgeous Smile and, encouraged by his approval, I say, 'I play a bit too.'

'Who for?'

'Um . . .' I am so tempted to tell him I play for Blackett because I want him to smile at me more, but I hesitate. Careful, Dani. If you say too much you'll let the cat out of the bag and you'll never get to play for them again. 'Oh, you know, I just kick a ball around with some of my mates.'

'Boy mates,' says Lissa reprovingly, but then she adds, 'She's really good.'

'You should join a ladies' team,' he says and then we launch into a debate on the merits of ladies' and mixed football over men's and after a while the others drift away, bored out of their skulls.

It turns out that Rupert is very knowledgeable about sport. He plays football for a Saturday league team as well as being captain of his school rugby team, plus he surfs and plays tennis in the summer and skis when he gets the chance. Action man! But he's really easy to talk to now I've got over my initial embarrassment.

I can't help noticing he's got nice eyes as well as a gorgeous smile.

'Can I get you a drink?' he asks and I say yes, feeling incredibly grown-up. I am really enjoying this party. I almost wish the Barbies were here to see me chatting away to this guy; that would be one in the eye for them with their patronizing remarks.

I sigh happily and glance around the room. Everyone looks as if they're enjoying themselves. I've been so engrossed in conversation with Rupert that I didn't notice Ajay arriving. He's chatting to Lissa and he's brought a friend with him.

Even from the back, there is something familiar about that friend.

I freeze. Oh no! I don't believe it!

It's Marvyn.

Chapter 16

Marvyn turns round and looks straight at me. I expect him to be shocked when he sees I'm a girl but he just grins at me so I grin back weakly. When he turns back to Lissa I can hardly breathe, waiting for her reaction. I am so dead.

But they carry on chatting as normal. He hasn't split on me. *Thank you, Marvyn. I owe you.*

When he looks back I smile again in gratitude, but this time his eyes pass right over me and continue sweeping the room, like he's looking around to see if he knows anyone else. And then the penny drops. He hasn't recognized me dressed as a girl. Why would he? He's only ever seen me before as a mud-splattered male footballer.

He glances at most girls without a blink but then he spots Tash, who is still talking to

Duncan, and nudges Ajay in the ribs. Ajay sees her too and his eyes light up and immediately he makes a beeline for her. Poor Lissa, she doesn't stand a chance.

She still trails after him though, so Marvyn, who is left on his own, follows her. I try to avoid eye contact as they pass but at the last minute I can't resist looking up. Marvyn catches my eye and grins again. Then he stops, a small frown appearing between his eyebrows. Oh no! Look down, Dani, look down!

'Do I know you?' he asks.

Um, yes. We've played football together.

'Don't think so,' I say breathily, my voice unnaturally high, trying desperately to model myself on the Barbies, the most girly-girls I know.

Convince him you're someone else, Dani. You can do it. Don't look him in the eye. Play with your hair. Show him your red-white-and-blue-striped fingernails. And smile. That's it.

'You remind me of someone,' he says thoughtfully. 'But I can't think who.'

Oh flip. Flutter your eyelashes! That's what Georgia does.

I open and close my eyes rapidly and he looks a bit alarmed, but stands his ground.

'Have you got something in your eye?'

'Some mascara. And eyeliner. You know, just girly stuff.' I giggle nervously.

'What's your name?' he asks.

'Danielle,' I mumble.

'What?'

'Dani-*elle*,' I repeat, emphasizing the Elle. It works.

'Hi, Elle, I'm Marvyn,' he says. 'Are you at school with Tash?'

I nod, groaning inwardly. He's going to find out, I know he is, and then I'm done for. I am going to be so humiliated when everyone finds out I've been pretending to be a boy. Plus my football career will be over before it's even started.

It's not fair. I am never going to live this down, especially when the Barbies get to hear about it!

And then I spot him. My superhero!

Rupert is coming to the rescue bearing two tall glasses containing some sort of sparkling drink decorated with umbrellas and pieces of fruit. I hear myself saying, 'Actually, I'm with someone. Have you met Rupert?' and I surprise myself because I sound so sophisticated.

Marvyn looks up and sees him too. 'Sorry, mate!' he mumbles and moves away.

It worked! I can handle this. I feel so grown-up.

'Who's your friend?' asks Rupert as he hands me the drink.

I smile at him mysteriously and take a large gulp while I think of a cool answer. I'm learning so fast!

'Easy,' says Rupert warningly. 'It's very fizzy.' But it's too late. The bubbles go straight up my nose and explode. He looks at me in alarm as I start snorting uncontrollably.

'Are you OK?'

I gasp for air as my nose makes loud pig noises. People turn round to look and start to giggle. Lissa comes over and bangs me unhelpfully on the back.

'Don't do that!' I splutter as snot emerges from my nose and drips unbecomingly on to my blue silk dress.

Correction, Lissa's blue silk shirt. Now she is looking at me with disgust and Rupert is staring at me in horror and I can't breathe.

The whole room is staring at me. Including Marvyn.

This party is turning into a disaster. There is no way I'm going to keep my cover if I'm the centre of attention like this. I need to get out of here quickly before Marvyn recognizes me and Incredible-Snorting-Pig-Girl is finally unmasked as Imposter-Boy-Footballer in front of everyone.

Including the first ever crush of her life, the gorgeous Rupert.

'Need the loo!'

I make a dash through my open-mouthed audience to the downstairs cloakroom, snorting all the way.

Chapter 17

'What happened to you Friday night?' says Lissa accusingly on Monday morning as she hands me my school bag in the yard.

I take a peek inside. My school uniform, my jeans and favourite T-shirt and my hockey kit have been washed and ironed to within an inch of their lives. They look brand new. I'm wearing my spare set of uniform today which looks nowhere near as smart.

I hand Lissa a plastic bag. She stares glumly down at its crumpled, snot-stained blue-silk contents. Oops! I should've asked my mum to wash her shirt/dress thing. I'm not like Lissa, I don't think of these things.

'It was the bubbles. They went up my nose. I couldn't help it.'

Tash giggles at the memory but Lissa gives

95

her a stern look and she stops immediately. She and Ali are standing slightly behind Lissa to the left and right like a deputation. Oh dear, I thought this might happen. I'd texted Lissa to let her know that I'd got home safely but after that I'd ignored their calls all weekend. I knew I'd have to face them this morning though.

Lissa: 'I don't mean that. I mean why did you run off . . .?'

Ali: 'Without saying goodbye to anyone . . .?'

Tash: 'Like Cinderella?'

I look with interest at Tash. I hadn't thought of it like that. I suppose it was a bit like a fairy tale with me (Cinderella) fleeing into the night away from Rupert (my handsome prince) with a secret I had to keep hidden at all costs. Only I'd left my muddy clothes behind instead of a jewelled slipper.

So what did that make them then? The Ugly Sisters!

I resist the urge to laugh but I can't have been very successful because Lissa snaps, 'It's not funny, Dani! You never even thanked my mum for the party!'

'I'm sorry!' I say genuinely.

'She thought we'd had an argument and you'd run off upset,' she continues.

'But we didn't –'

'*I* know that, but *she* didn't! I had to stop her from ringing your mum.'

'Oh flip!' My mum would be furious if she found out.

She scowls at me. 'And Rupert gave me grief too.'

'Did he?'

'Yeah. He said it must've been my fault you went home because when you were talking to him, you were getting on fine.'

'Did he? Did he really say that?'

'Yeah. I just said he did, didn't I? What's wrong with you?'

Even though I'd been dreading coming in this morning, I suddenly feel light and happy.

'I'm sorry!' I repeat and fling my arms round her neck. 'It was *so* embarrassing what with me snorting like a pig and snot pouring out of my nose and everyone in the party looking at me. I just wanted to go home. So when I came out of the loo and no one was looking, I grabbed my coat and made a dash for it.'

97

Lissa goes from prickly cross to soft and melty in two seconds flat. 'That's OK,' she says and pats me on the back. 'I get embarrassed sometimes too.'

'Yeah,' says Ali thoughtfully. 'But *Dani* embarrassed! That's got to be a first.'

'It's probably your hormones,' says Lissa kindly. 'That's what Mum says when I go moody.'

I want to tell her that's not hormones, that's her, because Lissa is renowned for being moody. But things are going so well I refrain and just nod in agreement.

'It was a great party though,' I say. 'Thanks for inviting me, Liss.' She beams at me. Then I can't resist adding, even though I know how risky it is, a bit like prodding a troublesome tooth to see if it's still aching, 'It was good to see Ajay and his friend there too.'

'Marvyn?' Lissa goes a bit dewy-eyed. 'He was nice, wasn't he?'

Tash squeals. 'I knew it! Lissa for Marvyn! Lissa for Marvyn! I saw you dancing with him at the end!' and Lissa goes red. Then Tash adds, 'I was chatting to him yesterday and he said he had a good time,' and Lissa goes redder still.

'Who was Elle by the way?' adds Tash and my heart does a somersault.

'Elle?' asks Lissa.

'Yeah. Only he said he'd been talking to someone called Elle at the party.'

'There wasn't anyone called Elle at the party,' repeats Lissa, puzzled, and then her face falls. 'Oh no! He must've meant Ella. I bet he fancies her! Didn't he mention me at all?'

'Yeah. Non-stop. He said you were the most beautiful girl he'd ever seen in his whole life and he was madly in love with you,' says Tash with a straight face.

Just for a split second you can see that Lissa believes her. Then, as Tash bursts out laughing, Lissa shrieks and swings the plastic bag with the blue shirt at her head and she ducks and runs off, with Lissa chasing her.

And then, thank goodness, the bell goes for school and Ali links her arm through mine and we go inside chuckling at them both and a new school week begins.

Chapter 18

If anything, Mrs Waters steps up the pace of hockey training this week. To tell the truth I'm loving it but not everyone feels the same. The weather continues to be cold and wet and some people cry off, pleading coughs and colds, such as Georgia, though it's pretty obvious there's nothing wrong with her. Even stalwarts like Lissa start to object when she slips and falls flat on her back in the mud.

'I'm soaked right through to my knickers!' she wails as we're getting changed afterwards. I make the mistake of laughing and she glares at me. 'It's not fair,' she grumbles. 'It's all right for you. *We're* going through all this for nothing. We don't even get the chance to try out for the development squad.'

'Shut up, Lissa. Dani's miles better than us,' says Tash, which only makes Lissa scowl more.

'We are the Gang of Four, the No Secrets Club, remember?' reminds Ali sternly. 'We have to support each other. Like you supported me for the fashion show.'

Ali is so loyal. She's not even in the hockey team but she's been turning out to play to plug the gaps.

Lissa looks a bit shamefaced. 'I know. Sorry, Dani.'

'It's OK. Don't worry.' I give her a hug. 'It'll be your turn next. Anyway, I might not even get in.'

'Course you will,' she says, hugging me back. Lissa might be moody but she never bears grudges. 'You better had,' she adds fiercely, 'after all this effort.'

'I'll do my best,' I say flatly. But the truth is I'm not even sure I want to. Well, I do, obviously; it would be brilliant to learn to play hockey at a higher level and Mum and Gran would be so proud of me. But I don't know how often this Development Centre thingy meets, and I'm guessing it's going to be on Saturdays. So how on earth am I going to manage that if I'm already playing football?

I give a big sigh and Ali looks at me strangely. 'Cheer up,' she says. 'I thought you loved hockey?'

'I do,' I say truthfully but I don't add the obvious. I love football more. It looks like I'm going to have some choices to make. I've got my first match for Blackett this weekend. I just can't see how I'm going to fit everything in.

Then, as if Lissa can read my mind and has decided to make my already complicated life even more stressful, she says, 'Hey, you lot! Don't forget we're meeting up this Saturday at Donatella's.'

'Are we?' I say blankly.

'Yeah. It's my birthday, remember?'

'It was your birthday last week,' I point out.

'Duh! That was my party, stupid. Anyway, you don't have to worry, it's my treat. My Auntie Florence sent me some money and I can't think of a better way of spending it than on coffee and cake with my three best friends.'

'Aahh! Thanks, Liss. That's really generous of you,' says Ali, smiling. 'I'll be there.'

Tash beams. 'Me too. So long as it's OK with my mum. Shouldn't be a problem,' she adds cheerfully.

'What about you, Dani?' asks Lissa pointedly. 'You are coming, aren't you?'

I hesitate and a hurt expression flashes across her face. She thinks I don't want to.

'You're playing football with your mates,' she says bitterly. 'Of course. Silly me.'

'Dann-nii,' whispers Ali disapprovingly.

'It's Lissa's birthday,' Tash points out, her usual smiley face serious for once.

'I can't,' I say weakly. 'I've got to go and see my gran.' Even to my ears it sounds like an excuse.

'Yeah, right,' says Lissa, her voice hollow. She doesn't believe me. None of them do. Three faces glare at me.

I swallow hard and do some rapid calculations in my head. 'I could come before though, if you want,' I say. 'For an hour.'

'YAY!' Lissa flings her arm round my neck. 'About eleven o'clock?'

'Ten,' I say. 'Ten would be better.'

But she doesn't respond. She's too busy gabbling away about the different coffees and cakes at Donatella's.

Chapter 19

The night before my first ever proper league football match I'm so excited I hardly sleep a wink. I'd gone to town after school that day and bought myself a new pair of football boots because my old ones from primary school were too small for me. They cost a bomb. Mum would have a fit if she knew I'd blown all my savings on them. But they're worth it.

The next morning I give Jade firm instructions. ('Meet me at the station in time to catch the five past eleven train and DON'T be late!') Then I leave the house with my sports bag packed and ready for the game, to go and meet the others first for our cake-date.

Donatella's is closed and there is no sign of anyone. I end up waiting outside, hopping impatiently from foot to foot, sending 'Where are you?' texts to my absent friends. At last Lissa responds.

On my way. Thought we were meeting at 11.

I groan aloud. Why does life always have to be so complicated? There's no way I can get in touch with Jade to tell her of the change of plan because she hasn't got a mobile and she'll have left the house by now. And, anyway, I don't want to miss the match!

Just as I'm debating whether I dare give up and make a bolt for it the shutters go up at last and everyone arrives more or less simultaneously. Lissa is excited, insisting we all choose a different cake so we can share, even though Ali and Tash both want the triple chocolate and I don't want any because I'm so nervous for my first match. Only I can't tell them that.

The waitress is really chatty, making lots of suggestions (Aagh! How can there be that many cakes in one little cafe?) and everyone keeps changing their minds and it takes FOREVER to order, though no one else seems to mind except me.

Then Lissa starts pulling out things from her bag to show us what she got for her birthday and Ali and Tash go 'Aahh!' and 'Oohh!' so I have to join in too otherwise it looks like I'm not interested. (I'm not actually, I hate smellies and jewellery and stuff.) And all the time that I'm 'Oohing' and 'Aahhing', I'm worrying about making it to the match in time. The cakes arrive at last and we all have to sing 'Happy Birthday' to Lissa and then Tash sings a rude version as well that her brother Devon taught her, which, I have to admit, is hilarious. But amid all this frivolity I keep checking my watch when no one's looking and wondering how quickly I can scoff my cake and make my exit.

The trouble is we still have to try each other's cakes because Lissa says so. And then, because she has to make *everything* a competition, we have to give marks for them out of ten and choose an overall winner. Naturally, this turns into a heated and prolonged argument because everyone has a different opinion, even though, actually, I don't give a stuff, it's just a bit of cake and I NEED TO GET GOING!

You see, I'm worried sick that the match will

start without me. I mean, if I can't turn up on time for the very first match, Terry will never ever pick me again. After all this effort, I'll have blown it before I even started!

In the end Lissa's cake is chosen as the best which I could've told you was going to happen in the first place and saved us all a lot of time and energy. At last I can spring to my feet.

'Got to go now, Liss,' I say in a rush. 'Sorry. Jade's waiting for me at the station. Thanks for the cake. It was brilliant.'

And even though I can see her face clouding over with disappointment I leg it as fast as I can before she has time to object.

She texts me. I knew she would. I can hear messages pinging on my phone as I'm running through the streets but I ignore them. All ten of them.

I arrive at the station, hot and sweaty and out of breath, and cast my eyes around for Jade. I spot her, sitting alone on a bench, her head in a book as usual. She looks up, first at me, then pointedly at the big station clock above us.

'You're late,' she says accusingly.

'Sorry!'

'You told me not to be, but you are. Nearly an hour late.'

'I know.' I swallow hard, grateful for my stoical younger sister. Mum would go mad if she knew I'd abandoned her at a train station on a busy Saturday morning. Most kids would've attracted attention by now, made a fuss, burst into tears and be surrounded by a crowd of concerned people wanting to take them into care.

Not Jade though. She'd just sat quietly, lost in her book, and no one even noticed.

'We've missed the train,' she points out.

'Come on. We'll get the next one,' I say, hoping we haven't missed that too. I glance up at the departures screen and see there's one waiting on the opposite platform. 'Quick! It's ready to go!'

We run across the bridge and jump on the train. As we sink into our seats I breathe a sigh of relief. Phew! I'm going to make it. Just.

'You're playing football this afternoon, aren't you?' says Jade the mind-reader.

'Might be.' I'm trying to sound non-committal but it doesn't quite come off. I take my phone out of my pocket and loads of messages flash up. Not just from Lissa, but from Ali and Tash too. What do they want?

'Why won't you tell anyone?' persists Jade.

'It's not a secret,' I protest.

'Yes it is. You don't even want Mum and Gran to know.'

I can hardly deny this after the episode in the park. Jade hasn't spilt the beans; she's not the kind to snitch. She peers out through the window as I open my first message from Lissa.

'Do *they* know?'

'Does who know?'

'Your friends.'

I look up and follow her gaze. Lissa, Ali and Tash are standing by the barriers. Ali spots me and points, and she and Tash jump up and down and wave madly. Lissa, in contrast, seems to be arguing heatedly with the guy in uniform.

What is going on? Surely they're not trying to get on the train as well? Please, please tell me they're not thinking of coming with us?

Lissa must've won her argument because the guy suddenly holds the barrier open and they all burst through. But my prayers are answered as our train lurches into motion and I breathe a sigh of relief and sit back, glancing down at the message on my phone that I've just opened.

You've forgotten your bag!

Too late, I jump to my feet. As the train pulls slowly away from the station, I see my three friends on the opposite platform, Lissa holding my sports bag containing my brand-new football boots up high like a trophy.

Chapter 20

First ever game for the Blackett Junior team.
I'm late and I have no kit. Great start.

'Here,' says Terry, flinging a pair of football
boots at me. 'Lucky for you I held on to the
new strip for the big day, that's all I can say.
Now get yourself changed and out on that field,
pronto!'

They're Ryan's old pair and about two sizes
too big for me but I'm in no position to be
picky. Everyone else is already changed and
warming up on the pitch. Blue and white shirt,
blue shorts, navy and blue socks. Very smart.
Supply your own boots – unless, like in my case,
you've left them on the train.

That was my story and I was sticking to it.
It was bad but not quite as bad as the truth.
'Sorry, Terry, I left my boots in a cafe where I

was having coffee and cake with my girl-mates. Oh yeah, did I tell you that's why I'm late for this mega-important match?'

Don't think that would've gone down too well with him somehow. Terry doesn't know what to make of me, I can tell. On the one hand, I'm one of the best players on the field. (I'm not boasting, it's true.) On the other hand, I turn up late for my first match, minus my boots, and I'm inconsistent. (As witnessed by him at the selection match, when I went to pieces. OK, I had good reason to; if my mum and gran had spotted me the game would be up – literally – but he didn't know that.) What's he supposed to think?

I dash into the changing rooms, which we are allowed to use today for the first time now we're an official team, and get my kit on. At least because I'm late I don't have to worry about changing in front of the others, something that I'd been fretting about quietly all week. Until now we've just played in the clothes we've turned up in. I slip into my shirt and shorts, loving the feel of their silky smoothness against my skin. Is that what the boys think too? Then, keeping my own socks on, I tug the others up and over them and lace up the boots. They'll do. They'll have to! A bit loose but I can manage. I straighten up, square my shoulders and take a deep breath.

This is it, Dani. You won't get a second chance. Now you have to go out there and prove to Uncle Terry and Ryan and Vikram and Lofty and Marvyn and all the others and, maybe, most of all, to yourself that you deserve a place in Blackett United Junior Football Team.

Can you do it?

I stumble over my outsize boots.

Yes, I can.

We take a little while to get the feel of the game, to get the feel of us playing together as a team. Vikram goes out like a bull at a gate, rampaging round everywhere, and is cautioned for diving. Ryan is the opposite, starting off so slow he's almost timid. My boots are a bit of a problem, but I soon get used to them. Gradually we settle down and slowly, imperceptibly we take control and are eventually rewarded by a brilliant header goal from Lofty. At half-time, we're one–nil up.

'Well done, boys,' says Terry as he passes

around bottles of water. 'But it's not over yet. Brilliant goal, Lofty – more of those please. Keep it up, Danny, you're playing well. Marvyn, we need more direction in midfield . . .'

Marvyn. I'd been a bit concerned last Saturday after the party that he'd recognized me. I was pretty sure a few times I'd caught him looking at me but he'd said nothing and today we have more important things to worry about.

'Your dad here?' whispers Lofty. I shake my head and turn to survey the people who've gathered to watch us. It was quite an impressive number.

'Mine is. You can't miss him.' I follow his gaze to where a tall lanky guy is standing head and shoulders above the rest of the crowd and gulp. Even though he's not wearing his trademark cord jacket, only one person could possibly be that tall.

Mr Little.

'Is that your dad?'

'Afraid so.'

Mr Little sees me watching him and waves. Oh no, he's recognized me! That's all I need. After my monumental efforts my cover is about to be blown by a beanpole supply teacher who happens to be a dad. Then, beside me, Lofty waves back and I realize it's him he's waving at, not me, and I'm struck by how proud he looks of his son. And I can't help wishing my dad was here to be proud of me too.

But there's no time to think about that because the second half is about to start and we've got a job to do.

And we do it. Beautifully. Basically, with a lot of skill and a little good fortune, we run rings round the opposition. With increasing confidence we gradually seize possession and territory, and though they hold out and manage a goal somewhere along the way, it's not enough. Systematically we slaughter them: four goals to one.

And I score two of them, even in boots two sizes too big for me. It's magic.

Terry is over the moon. We all are. Mr Little and the other dads go wild on the touchline, jumping and shouting like it's the FA Cup Final. Our very first fixture and we've stolen the show.

We head back to the changing rooms in a blaze of glory, arms wrapped round each other.

'Leave your kit here and I'll take it home and

wash it for you,' orders Terry. 'Don't want anyone leaving it behind next week like Dopey Danny here.' He ruffles my hair to show he doesn't mean it as people start tugging their shirts over their heads and dropping them into Terry's big bag. 'And don't forget to shower, you lot, before you disappear to your parents.'

Everyone groans but does as they're told. I avert my eyes as boys pull off their kit and make a dash for the showers. I'd been dreading this.

'What's the problem, Danny?' asks Terry, noticing my hesitance.

'Haven't got a towel. Left it on the train, didn't I?' He will never know how grateful I am for forgetting my bag at this point in time.

'Go on!' he scoffs. 'Someone'll lend you theirs.' I bite my lip, wondering what on earth I can say to get out of this, and he adds, 'I don't want your dad after me for sending you home dirty.'

'My dad couldn't care less,' I say bitterly. 'He doesn't live with us any more.'

'What about your mum?'

'She's at work. I can have a shower before she gets home.'

He hesitates. 'No one watching you today then?'

I shake my head.

His eyes soften and he gives me a wry smile. 'Pity,' he says gently. 'You did well. Your parents would be proud of you.' Then he ruffles my hair again.

'Go on then!' he says, his voice back to normal. 'Get off home and tell your mum how well you played. See you next week, Danny. And don't forget your boots!'

'I won't!' I say happily and get changed quickly before someone comes out of the showers and offers to lend me their towel.

I'd got away with it this time. But how would I manage next week?

Chapter 21

'This is becoming a habit!'

As Lissa hands me my bag on Monday morning I can't help noticing how cross and disapproving she looks.

This isn't actually that unusual for Lissa. But it is for Ali and Tash who are looking cross and disapproving too.

'What's wrong?'

'Thought you were going to see your grandmother on Saturday?' says Lissa.

'I was.' Correction. 'I did.'

It was true. I had seen Gran. Briefly. For the first time ever since we'd been visiting her I'd gone straight to the park when I got off the train and sent Jade along to Gran's on her own.

I'd had to. I had no choice; the match was about to start.

Two hours later, when the match was over, I'd arrived at Gran's house on cloud nine. But straight away I knew something was wrong. She was on the doorstep waiting for me with her arms folded and her first words brought me right back down to earth.

'Where have you been all this time?'

'The park! I told Jade to tell you where I was.'

'What are you getting up to down there for hours on end? You're not getting into bad company, are you?'

'No!' I darted a look at Jade, wondering if she'd said something. It wasn't like Gran to play the heavy guy.

But Gran must've seen the look because immediately she said, 'I'm responsible for you two when you're here, you know. If you're up to no good, I'll have your mother to answer to.'

I knew Mum coming up here last week was a bad idea. Now Gran had realized she'd been allowing me a bit too much freedom.

'*I'm* not up to no good!' Jade said indignantly. 'I came straight here. It's not my fault.'

'Neither am I,' I retorted quickly. 'I've just been hanging out with a few mates, that's all, Gran.'

'What do you mean by "mates"? Girls?'

Jade snorted at that point and my cover was blown. Though, to be fair, she did try to turn it (unsuccessfully) into a cough.

'Boys, actually,' I finally admitted. There was no point in lying for the sake of it.

When I sat at the table for my lunch Gran plonked a plate of fossilized cottage pie down in front of me. 'Don't blame me if it's spoiled. It's been in the oven for hours,' she snapped and sat down opposite me. Now I knew I was in for the third degree.

'Mmmm! Yummy!' I forked dried-up minced beef and peas as hard as bullets into my mouth, trying to distract her. 'This is delicious, Gran!' There was no fooling her though.

'You know, Dani, I think I'm going to have a word with your mother. I'm not sure she, or your father for that matter, would be happy to know that you're coming up to Blackett on the pretext of seeing me in order to meet up with boys in the park.'

'I'm not meeting up with boys in the park!'

I said, my face fiery red. 'Not like that, anyway.' What does she think I'm getting up to? That would be the Barbies' idea of heaven, not mine! 'I don't like boys, not the way you mean. I was just playing football with them, that's all.'

'Really?' She studied me carefully. 'So why all the secrecy?'

How do you tell your grandmother you've been passing yourself off as a boy? 'There is no secrecy!' I lied wildly. 'I just kick a ball around with them. We're mates.'

She gave me a suspicious look. 'That's all right then. Maybe we'll come along and watch you next week, shall we, Jade?'

Jade looked nervously at me. She didn't know what to say.

'It's not a proper match,' I protested. More lies. 'It'll be really boring.'

'Let me be the judge of that,' she said. 'Now eat up your lunch.'

I tried but it was hard to force down. Not because it was burned but because I could tell that she didn't believe a word I was saying. And when she found out the truth I had no idea what would happen next.

*

122

And now it's Monday morning and I've got three more accusing faces glaring at me.

Lissa (pointedly): 'Oh really? You went to visit your gran? Play football, does she?'

Me (defensive): 'Why d'you say that?'

Ali: 'Because inside your bag is a pair of football boots.'

Me (weakly): 'Is there?'

Tash: 'You know there is.'

Me (changing tack, sounding affronted): 'You looked then?'

Lissa: 'We were trying to do you a favour, Dani. Return it to you.'

Ali: 'In case you thought you'd lost it.'

Tash: 'We tried to phone you —'

Lissa: 'But you wouldn't answer.'

Me (in excuse): 'I was rushing to catch the train —'

Ali: 'So we looked in your bag to see if your phone was in there —'

Tash: 'And that's when we saw the football boots.'

Lissa: 'It was pretty obvious you'd gone off to play football —'

Ali: 'And you didn't want to talk to us.'

Me (telling a lie): 'It wasn't like that!'

Tash (telling the truth): 'Actually, we were a bit cross about it —'

Ali (kindly): 'But we knew you'd need the boots anyway —'

Lissa: 'And that's why we chased after you to the station.'

Ali: 'To give you your bag. That's all.'

Tash: 'Because we're still the Gang of Four —'

Ali: 'The No Secrets Club.'

Lissa (reprovingly): 'Even if you have been lying to us.'

Me (mortified, taking the bag from Lissa's out-stretched hand): 'Thanks. I don't know what to say. You are the best mates anyone could ever have. I really don't deserve this . . .'

But the bell has gone and everyone is flooding into school.

And nobody waits for me.

Chapter 22

First lesson, double PE. Unusually for her, Mrs Waters comes into the changing rooms in a tizz, clutching an open folder.

'Dani, I've just realized I need to get you into the Junior Development squad by the end of the month so you have a chance of making it to the Regional Performance Centre next year.'

At least, that's what I think she says. It's difficult to tell because she's rifling through the folder and muttering to herself behind clenched teeth. I catch some of what she's saying.

'How did I miss that? Need to keep on top of things . . . Still, shouldn't be a problem . . . She's ready . . . Should've realized the date . . . This term's going so fast . . . Could wait till next year . . . Be a shame though . . . Waste of talent . . .'

I wait patiently until finally she snaps the folder shut and fixes me with her beady eye. 'Right,' she says decisively, 'we need you up at the all-weather pitch at Crowley School on Saturday afternoon for a trial.'

My heart sinks. 'This Saturday, Miss?'

'Yes. Is that a problem?'

I hesitate and my eyes shift away from hers. Lissa is rolling hers at Tash and Ali. They know what's going through my mind. Football.

They don't know how important it is though. My second match for Blackett Juniors. I'm their chief striker. They need me.

Mrs Waters is waiting for an answer but I don't know what to say. Suddenly she explodes.

'Danielle! Why do you even need to think about this? I don't think you understand what an opportunity you could be missing.'

'I do, Miss!'

'We've been training a long time to get you ready for this trial.'

'I know, Miss.'

'Then, whatever you've got on this weekend, cancel it!'

Silence. Mrs Waters glares at me.

'Do you understand what an honour this is?'

'Yes, Miss.' I really do. I understand that if I get into the Junior Development Centre I can progress to the Regional Performance Centre and from there I might even go on to play hockey at national level one day. It's an incredible opportunity, one that most girls would give anything for.

Girls like Lissa and Tash, and poor old Ali who hadn't even made it into the Year Seven school team, and all the rest of them who'd turned out for weeks for me in the wind and rain to give me a chance to get into this elite group.

I was the high-flyer at sport, Mrs Waters' blue-eyed girl. The one who'd won the sports scholarship. I was meant to represent Riverside Academy at hockey and netball and any other sport under the sun. I would be letting down so many people if I didn't turn up for this hockey trial on Saturday.

Everyone is silent and I can feel the hostility radiating from my teacher and every other person in the room as they stand there glaring at me. Including my best mates. The Barbies are loving it.

'I really want to be in it, Mrs Waters,' I say humbly and I mean it.

'I should think so too!' she snaps. 'Be at Crowley School three o'clock sharp on Saturday. And don't be late.' She turns to Lissa, Tash and Ali. 'You lot, the rest of the Gang of Four. You're responsible for making sure she's there, right?'

'Yes, Miss,' they chorus.

'Don't let me down!' she barks. 'You don't seem to realize, Dani, you could go all the way with your talent. All you need is commitment.'

I gasp at the unfairness of it all. My problem is I am already committed. But I can't tell her that. I can't tell anyone. It's too late for that.

We go out on the field and she puts us through our paces so fast people don't know what's hit them. Chantelle says she thinks she's having a heart attack but Mrs Waters says a run round the field is the best cure for cardiac arrest (which I don't think is strictly true) and makes her do two laps. Then Zadie says she's pulled a muscle and she makes her run a lap backwards to make it better, but from Zadie's face I don't think it does. And she's really hard on everyone, especially me.

When we get back into the changing rooms

everyone blames me for our hockey lesson turning into some kind of boot camp.

'It's not my fault Mrs Waters was in a bad mood,' I protest as we get changed.

'Yes it is!' says Lissa grumpily. 'And now we've missed break and I'm starving!'

Then in French she says she doesn't feel well and so I suppose that's my fault too. Mrs Waters would've told her to go for a run but Madame Dupré is kinder than that and sends her to sick bay. We rush off to see her at lunchtime but to our surprise we discover that she's already gone home.

'Her mother came to collect her,' explains the secretary in Reception.

'Mrs Hamilton is such a fusspot,' says Ali as we make our way outside to our favourite bench.

'She couldn't have been that bad,' I say, puzzled. 'She said she was hungry. You don't feel like eating if you're sick.'

'She did look a bit pale and clammy though,' says Tash.

We sit down and open our packed lunches. It doesn't feel right, just three of us – it's not enough. The Barbies are a threesome; we're the Gang of Four. Lissa should be here investigating our lunchboxes, trying to swap her healthy-eating options for our sweet treats. She gets on my nerves sometimes but I wish she was here now to take my mind off things.

I don't know what to do about Saturday. I take a bite of my ham sandwich and start to mull it over.

It's always been football for me – my whole life, as long as I can remember. It should be straightforward. The fact that I, Danielle Jarvis, was actually playing Junior League football in a boys' team and making a success of it was my dream come true.

And I couldn't let them down.

But hockey was a good game too. The more I played it, the more I grew to love it.

Mrs Waters had said I was talented, that I could go all the way. She meant that I could represent not just my school, but my county, and one day my country if I worked hard enough.

She'd also said I lacked commitment. That hurt.

I couldn't let her and my friends down either.

How could I possibly choose between them?

A vision of World Cups and Olympic stadiums

drifts before my eyes. Me, the captain of the winning team, receiving the trophy, holding it up high to tumultuous cheers from the crowd. Football team or hockey team? Difficult to tell. There's a gold medal round my neck, the National Anthem is playing, Mum and Dad are standing shoulder to shoulder, beaming with pride –

'Dani!' A voice slices through my dreams. 'Hurry up and finish that sandwich. I want you out on the field in ten seconds flat.'

'Yes, Mrs Waters.' I take a final bite and wash it down with a swig of water.

'D'you want us too, Miss?' asks Tash, getting to her feet.

'No, I don't need you any more,' says Mrs Waters. 'Thanks for all your help but it's just down to you now, Dani. We're going to practise those skills till they're perfect.'

So that's what we do for the rest of the week. I don't see Tash and Ali except in lessons. I don't see Lissa at all because she's not well and stays at home for a few days. Every spare minute, breaktime, lunchtime and after school, Mrs Waters and I practise controlling the ball, passing, receiving, dribbling, turning, defending and shooting in scores of different drills repeated over and over again until I can do them in my sleep.

By Thursday night I'm as ready as I'm ever going to be to try out for the Junior Development Centre.

The only problem is I still don't know if I can get there.

Chapter 23

I toss and turn all night long and by Friday morning I've come to a decision.

I can't choose between playing football or hockey, it's impossible. I love them both. And, contrary to what Mrs Waters may think, I'm committed to them both.

So here's the thing. I'm going for both. It's the obvious solution. *If* I can pull it off.

I've worked out a plan. Tomorrow the footie match kicks off at 1 p.m. Half an hour each way because we're under twelve. I've just got enough time if I nip off quickly after the match to get the train straight back from Blackett and be up at Crowley School for three o'clock.

As part of that plan I tell Mum at breakfast that I'm not going to Gran's tomorrow.

'I want to meet my friends in town so we can

go to hockey together,' I say, my fingers tightly crossed against the lie. 'Hope you don't mind, Jade. They're coming along to support me, you see.'

Behind Mum's back Jade does that raised eyebrows thing which means, *What are you up to now?*

'What nice friends you've got,' says Mum. 'I'm not working tomorrow so Jade and I can come too. Where did you say it was?'

'Crowley School, three o'clock.'

'Don't forget to let your Gran know you won't be seeing her this weekend.'

'I will.'

So far, so good. Plot working. I won't have to waste time going to see Gran (sorry, Gran, nothing personal) and, even more important, *she* won't walk down to the park to see who I'm playing football with like she threatened to. She'll think I'm in town with my friends.

Now I've just got to tell Ali and Tash and Lissa (who's back at school today, right as rain again) the opposite: that I can't meet them in the morning because I'm going to see my gran. I never knew I could be such a good liar. It helps that at break and lunchtime I'm busy training with Mrs Waters, and then she takes me out of my last lesson for a pep talk, so it's the end of the day when I finally manage to catch up with them back in our classroom. They're in a huddle and they look as if they're making plans of their own.

'See you tomorrow!' I trill, popping my head round the door. 'At the hockey trial!'

The three of them jump apart. 'We were just talking about you,' says Tash. What a surprise. 'We were going to phone you,' she continues, 'to make arrangements.'

'What arrangements?' I ask, my heart sinking.

'We thought we'd all meet up first.'

'Meet up?'

'Yep. At the cafe,' says Ali. 'About eleven?'

'Eleven?'

'Yeah,' says Lissa. 'We could hang out, the four of us, have lunch, then go up to Crowley School for your hockey trial. Together.'

'Aahh, sorry, can't make it,' I say, trying to look regretful. 'What a shame. I'm going to my gran's in the morning as usual so I'll see you up at hockey.'

Three sets of eyes stare at me. Then Lissa says flatly, 'No way!'

I knew *she'd* try to sabotage my carefully thought-out scheme. But then Ali joins in as well.

'Mrs Waters told us we're responsible for getting you there, Dani,' she says. 'I think we should meet up first. Just to be on the safe side.'

'I'm not going to run away!' I laugh. 'I actually do want to get into the centre, you know!'

But Ali doesn't laugh back. Instead she exchanges a look with the others. I know what that look means. It says, louder than words, *She's going to play football.*

'I've got to see Gran first, poor old thing,' I protest. 'She looks forward to Saturdays when Jade and I visit her. She doesn't get out much and sometimes she sees no one all week long.' I pile it on thick, substituting the picture in my head of my busy, energetic Gran with one of a sad, lonely old lady, and adopt a suitably virtuous expression.

Tash studies me silently which is, weirdly, more unnerving than the others' objections. I wonder what is going on in her head.

'I'll be there!' I appeal to her, even though she hasn't said anything. 'Trust me! I don't want to let anyone down.'

'I know,' she says and gives me a sad little smile.

She believes me.

But she thinks I will anyway.

Chapter 24

Saturday dawns bright and sunny.

Part of me is excited.

Part of me wishes it was pouring with rain. Then the football would've been called off, but the hockey could still have gone ahead because it's on an all-weather pitch. I'd have done it properly then. I could've concentrated on doing Mrs Waters and Riverside Academy proud instead of being sick with nerves.

What happens if my plan fails? It could fall apart so easily. All it would take would be for the footie match to be delayed and I'd miss the hockey trial. Then everyone would hate me.

I'd hate me too.

I leave the house at the crack of dawn (at least that's what it feels like), determined to be on time for football at least. I catch an earlier train than usual and I've got a carriage to myself. I find myself wishing Jade was here with me.

'You're going to play football first, aren't you?' she'd whispered as I'd left the house. I'd nodded and she'd given me a hug. 'Don't be late for the trial!'

As the train trundles its way to Blackett I find myself staring gloomily out of the window and chewing the skin round my nails.

Stop it! I tell myself sternly. *What's wrong with you? You've got everything you ever wanted. You're an eleven-year-old girl and not only are you playing league football in a class boys' team but today you are trying out for what is effectively a place in the county hockey squad. What more do you want? You should be over the moon.*

But I'm not. In fact, I feel decidedly *under* the moon. And alone. And empty.

I've just discovered a truth about life.

Even if you get exactly what you want, it's not much fun unless you've got someone to share it with.

I mean, Jade doesn't really count. She doesn't understand football so she has no idea what a big deal it is for me to be in the Blackett team.

It's my own fault. I've deliberately played it down so she won't say anything to anyone.

It's my friends I want to tell: Lissa and Ali and Tash. I hate all this lying and pretence and subterfuge. I want them to be there watching me, cheering me on. I want them to see why football means so much to me. I want them to be proud of me.

And I want someone else to be proud of me too.

My dad.

Chapter 25

I'm not the only one who's early. Most people are already in the changing room. Our strip is there laid out ready for us, washed and pressed. Quickly I tug my hoody off and pull my shirt on over my T-shirt.

Next to me, Ryan gives me a funny look. 'What you doing?'

'I'm freezing,' I say, offering up a prayer of thanks that, unlike Lissa and Tash, I have absolutely no need whatsoever to wear a bra yet. Then I notice he's still staring at me. 'What?'

'Are you OK?'

'Yeah. Of course I am.'

'There's nothing wrong, is there?'

'What do you mean?'

'Well . . .' He looks a bit uncomfortable. 'Why are you freezing when it's not even cold?'

'I dunno . . .'

'And . . .' He hesitates and then blurts out, 'How come most of the time you're brilliant on the field, but sometimes you're rubbish?'

'Thanks!' I say, stung to the core. 'That was once! And it was because my mum nearly caught me!'

'Yeah, well that's the other thing! Why aren't you supposed to be playing football? What's the big secret, Danny?'

I stop, scared where this conversation is leading, and glance around but no one's listening. Ryan continues to stare at me, his face full of concern. 'You're not ill, are you?'

I'm so relieved, I burst out laughing.

'No, I'm fine. My mum's just a fusspot, that's all.' (*Sorry, Mum, that is so untrue.*)

Ryan's face clears. 'You're a weirdo!'

'*You're* a weirdo!'

'*You* are!'

We grin at each other. It sounds like a compliment.

Then, as Ryan laces up his boots, I tug my tracky pants off beneath my football shirt which conveniently drowns me and slip on my shorts. No one notices a thing. Again I'm aware of their silky softness but just in time stop myself commenting on it to Ryan. Now *that*, he would think, was definitely weird.

Pretending to be a boy is a minefield. Don't even think about the showers, Dani. Just concentrate on the job in hand. Beating the opposition.

The other team arrives on time and we go outside for a warm-up. All going to plan. I can feel myself relaxing. What could possibly go wrong? Soon the whistle blows and the game begins. This team is bigger and better than last week's and seems to be particularly dangerous down the right side of midfield where a boy built like a tank is marking me.

We get into our stride though and it's not long before a swift pass from Marvyn allows me to place the ball deep into the back of the net. A cheer goes up from the touchline and my heart lifts. I love this. The pace picks up as the other team goes into attack. We manage to hold them off with some good defensive work but it's not enough. By half-time, it's one all.

We're raring to go again in the second half and so are they. I run back on to the pitch and skip sideways while I wait for the game to restart, repeating Terry's advice like a mantra to myself: 'Keep in position. Don't let them through. Keep in position. Don't let them through . . .'

My voice trails away as I see someone striding down the hill towards us. Someone with short grey spiky hair and a flowing skirt, with a scarf trailing behind her like a flag. Unmistakeable. I can practically hear the beads and bangles jangling from here.

It's Gran.

My blood runs cold. What's she doing here? And then I remember, too late, I was supposed to ring her to cancel. With so much on my mind I'd completely forgotten. She must've been waiting for us to arrive for our usual visit and worrying where we'd got to. She knew where to find me though and now she was on the warpath.

'Dani!' she yells as she charges up to the pitch. 'Come here! I want a word with you!' Terry stares at her in surprise and Ryan and the others start laughing.

'Who's that?' asks Marvyn.

'My gran,' I say through gritted teeth. But he's not listening. He's been distracted by the sight of three more figures running towards us. Oh no! I don't believe it!

'Hey!' he says, his face lighting up. 'That's Tash. What's she doing here?'

'Don't know,' I bluff. 'Who's Tash?'

'She lives near my cousin Ajay,' he explains. 'She goes to that posh girls' school, Riverside Academy. See that girl with her, the tall one. Her name's Lissa. I went to her party a few weeks ago. There was loads of posh totty there.'

'I fancy the one with long dark hair,' says Ryan, looking at Ali.

'The tall one's not bad,' says Lofty.

'I fancy Tash,' says Marvyn. 'Everyone does. But Ajay's going out with her.'

Is he? I watch as Tash comes to a halt and spots Mr Little on the touchline. She points him out to the others and the three of them make their way over towards him.

Beside me Marvyn says, 'Actually, I fancy her mate as well.' So Lissa is in with a chance after all. But then he adds, 'She's called Elle, but she's going out with Lissa's brother. He's a right prat.' My face floods with heat but he's too busy looking at the girls to notice. 'I wonder where she is today?' he adds thoughtfully.

'Hey, Lofty. They're talking to your old man,' says Ryan. 'How do they know him?'

'Dunno.' Lofty frowns, then his face clears. 'Oh yeah. He's teaching on supply at Riverside Academy.'

'Give him a wave!' says Ryan, who's desperate to attract their attention.

'Hi, Dad!' calls Lofty obligingly. Mr Little and my three friends look up. Lissa's jaw drops a mile as she takes in first me and then Marvyn. Automatically she raises her hand and waves back, then the three of them start gesticulating to us.

Lofty is made up. 'Yay! Think I'm in there,' he says, looking pleased with himself. But it's not him they're calling over, it's me. And my three friends are not the only ones after my blood.

'Dani!' shouts my grandmother at the top of her voice, looking like she's about to march on to the field and grab me. 'Do you think I've got nothing better to do with my life than chase after you? Come here this minute!'

Lissa, Ali and Tash turn to stare at her,

open-mouthed. Terry, in alarm, moves over to see what the matter is and takes her by the arm to calm her down. Gran shakes him off.

'I JUST WANT A WORD WITH MY GRANDDAUGHTER!' she roars.

As I register the shock on Terry's face – on everyone's face – I groan. The game's up. My secret world is imploding. I close my eyes and wait for his voice to order me off the pitch in front of everyone.

Oh, the shame of it! Can you be arrested for impersonating a boy? You can for impersonating a policeman.

But then, suddenly, the whistle blows for the start of the second half, and my eyes burst wide open again. What's the point of worrying about anything or anyone any more? My cover is blown. But until someone tells me to get off this field, I've still got a job to do. And if this is the last chance I'm ever going to get to play for a decent team, then I'm going to make the most of it. What have I got to lose?

I play like a person possessed. I come out attacking and no one can stand in my way. Tank Boy doesn't stand a chance. Three minutes into the game and I've scored.

Two–one. The crowd goes wild.

Not long after, an exquisite cross from me (no time for false modesty) allows Ryan to head the ball into the net and take the credit.

Three–one. I can even hear Gran cheering.

Then the other team steps up their game. Fifteen minutes of hard play and finally they manage a goal kicked low into the net.

Three–two.

They've regained their confidence now. We've hardly had time to reassemble properly before they've done it again with a cheeky header.

Three all.

The crowd is behind us, spurring us on. 'BLACK-ETT! BLACK-ETT! BLACK-ETT!' It sounds huge, but they're just a blur.

I'm on the halfway line. We've got to be down to the last few minutes of the game. I take possession of the ball and see Tank Boy bearing down on me and feel a flash of panic. He's twice the size of me. Get rid of it quick!

'Take your time, Dani! Don't rush it!'

It's strange. I can hear my father's voice as clear as a bell, like he's standing here in the crowd, watching me and willing me on. All that practice, all those words of advice he gave me over the years. *Calm down*, I tell myself. *You can do this.*

I size up the distance, the angle, the possibility, just like my dad taught me, then pull my leg back and take an almighty kick at goal. The ball leaves the side of my foot and soars up high into the air and comes down in a perfect arc to rest in the back of the net.

'GOOOOOOOOAAAAAAAAAAAAAAAA AAAAALLLLLLLLLL!!!!!!!!!!!!!!!!!!!!!!!!!!!!!'

Four–three. And my first hat-trick.

The whistle blows for the end of the game.

Job done.

Chapter 26

I sink to the ground, exhausted. My teammates pile on top of me, yelling and cheering. When they finally let me go I can hardly stand up. Then I discover that some of the crowd have run on to the pitch and want a piece of me too.

Lissa, Ali and Tash are hanging off my neck, jumping up and down with excitement.

'DAN-NI! DAN-NI! DAN-NI!' yells Tash.

'We never knew you were that good!' screams Ali.

'Awesome!' agrees Lissa, her eyes shining. 'You're the best.'

'What are you doing here?'

'We bumped into your mum and Jade this morning in town,' explains Tash.

'Yeah,' says Ali. 'Your mum thought you were with us.'

'Jade fessed up so we all jumped on the train to Blackett to make sure you made it back in time for the hockey trial,' says Lissa. 'We're your police escort.'

'All? You mean . . .'

'Your mum's over there. With Jade.'

I turn to see them on the touchline and breathe a sigh of relief as Mum waves at me. It's OK, she's smiling. Beside her, Mr Little gives me the thumbs-up.

'Is that really your gran?' asks Ali. 'I thought she was supposed to be a frail old lady.'

'Oh flip!' Gran is bearing down on me. She doesn't look in the slightest like a frail old lady; she's more scary than Tank Boy. But instead of telling me off, she flings her arms round me and hugs me so tight I can't breathe.

'I'm so proud of you!' she says.

Squashed up against her, eyes closed, my nose pressed into her neck, I hear a familiar voice.

'Me too.'

That's all he says. But I'd know his voice anywhere. My eyes shoot open.

It's my dad. He's really here.

Chapter 27

We make it to the hockey trial just in time.

Lissa's right. They are like a police escort. I'm in Dad's car with Mum, Jade and Gran. Mr Little's car is in front of us with Lissa, Tash and Ali. Uncle Terry brings up the rear with Ryan, Lofty and Marvyn. Nobody wants to miss it, you see.

I sit in the passenger seat next to my dad.

'Should've told you I was coming,' he says apologetically. 'I just came on spec see, cos I knew you've been visiting your gran on Saturdays. It's been a while since I caught up with you and Jade. But when I turned up, there was no one there.'

'I was out looking for her,' pipes up Gran. 'I was wondering where she'd got to.'

'I *told* you to ring Gran and tell her you weren't coming!' Mum scolds me from the back seat.

'Sorry!'

'I knew where she'd be though. Playing football with the boys!' chuckles Gran. 'She's a chip off the old block, David.'

'Playing for Blackett, just like your old man!' Dad shakes his head in disbelief. 'Who'd have thought it? And Terry Jeeves coaching you! No wonder you're all so good. He used to be skipper of the Wanderers years ago.'

'They won't want me playing with them any more,' I grumble. 'Not now they know I'm a girl. All thanks to you, Gran.'

'Course they will,' he chuckles. 'You're their star player. You've earned your place in that team. They won't want to see you go.'

And you know something? Dad's right. When Terry's car pulls into Crowley School behind us, Ryan jumps out and comes running over to bang on my window.

'It's OK,' he says, breathless with excitement. 'Uncle Terry says it's OK. There's nothing in the rules that says you can't play for us.'

'D'you still want me to?' I ask shyly.

'Yeah.' He looks at me as if I'm mad. 'Course we do.'

I look back at my dad and he winks at me. 'See?' he says softly. 'What did I tell you?'

It's great to have the boys there cheering me on. Though I suspect the real reason they're so keen to come along and watch me play hockey is they get to hang out with Ali, Lissa and Tash. It's awesome to have my three best mates there too, plus Mum and Dad and Jade and Gran and Terry as well. Not to forget Mrs Waters. My very own supporters' club!

The game is tough, the standard huge, but hearing them all shouting for me helps me conquer my nerves. By the end of the game the team I'm on is beaten, two–one, but it was me that scored for our side with a reverse stick shot into the top corner.

I do it. I get into the Junior Development Centre.

All my dreams come true in one day! Everyone crowds around, congratulating me.

'Never knew you had such a fan club, Dani,' says Mrs Waters, laughing. When Uncle Terry tells her the tale of me playing football for Blackett, she can't believe her ears. Her jaw drops, then she puts her hands on her hips and regards me sternly. Oh flip!

'So what happens now, young lady?'

'What do you mean, Miss?' I ask, quaking in my boots.

'Well, you've got a choice to make. Are you going to be a top-class football player or a top-class hockey player?'

Everyone is looking at me.

I gulp. That's the crucial question. How do I choose between them? I look at my three best friends all waiting for me to reply.

It's like asking me to choose between Ali, Tash and Lissa. Which one do I like best? It's impossible.

'I don't know,' I say sadly.

She bursts out laughing. 'Don't look so worried, I'm only teasing you.'

'But, Miss, you're right. I can't play both football and hockey, can I?'

'Why not?'

'Because I can't fit it all in. It was a real rush today and I got a lift. If I have to get a train every week I'll be late for hockey and –'

'Whoa!' She holds up both hands. 'The Junior

Development squad meets for training on Monday nights –'

'And *we* play on Saturdays,' says Terry.

'So what's the problem?' asks Mrs Waters, and they smile at each other.

'There isn't one,' I say, smiling too.

And you know something?

There really isn't.

Chapter 28

'So, Sports Diva Extraordinaire, do you think you can find time to occasionally squeeze us into to your busy life?' says Lissa sarcastically. But she budges up to let me sit down next to her on the bench, checking out the contents of my lunchbox with interest. 'Mmm. Swap you my chicken salad wrap for your sponge cake?'

Monday lunchtime: usual gang, usual place. The Barbies are hanging around, trying to earwig our conversation. They've caught wind of what happened at the weekend. They don't frighten me; I've got nothing to hide any more. I give them a dirty look, Lissa-style, and it works. They fade away, affronted.

'I'm not a diva,' I protest, shielding my slice of cake from her prying fingers. 'Get your hands off!'

'No, you're not,' says Tash. 'I knew you'd never deliberately let anyone down.' She, more than anyone, knows what it's like to try to be in two places at once.

'I don't know how you got away with it for so long,' says Lissa admiringly. 'Didn't anyone in that football team of yours ever guess that you were a girl?'

'No. Nobody. I was a bit worried about Marvyn after your party but even he didn't recognize me. Ryan thought I was weird though.'

'Why?'

'Loads of reasons. But mainly because he saw me putting my football shirt on over my clothes.' They all look at me in surprise and I explain, 'Well, I could hardly strip off in front of him, could I?' and they start giggling.

'Oh, I wish I'd been there,' says Tash.

'Yeah, why didn't you tell us?' asks Ali. 'We're your mates.'

'The Gang of Four,' says Lissa.

'The No Secrets Club,' says Tash.

We look at each other and burst out laughing.

'Maybe,' I point out, 'it's time to change our name to the Secrets Club.'

'It'll be you next, Lissa,' says Ali, kindly handing her half of her blueberry muffin. 'What's your big secret? Here you are, greedy guts. You're like Oliver, always asking for more.'

'No I'm not,' says Lissa. 'It's just that you lot have nicer treats than I do.'

'Yeah, right,' I say, raising a suitably sardonic eyebrow. 'Remember your birthday party?'

'Yes, *Elle*,' says Tash meaningfully, and they all start giggling again. I can feel my colour rising.

'I meant the food!' I protest, but it's too late.

'Marvyn was quite taken with you that night if I remember rightly,' Tash persists.

'Yeah, till he found out I was a boy!' I say, and Lissa chokes, spluttering muffin crumbs everywhere.

I thump her on the back. 'It was sooooo embarrassing!' I admit, recalling Marvyn's face on Saturday when Danny, lead striker for Blackett Juniors, was finally exposed as Danielle, Year Seven girl from Riverside Academy. I mean, everyone was surprised, but for him it was worse, much worse. Because I could see that the penny had suddenly dropped.

'I don't know if I should tell you lot this or not . . .'

'Tell us!'

'No secrets, remember?'

'We-ell . . . so long as you promise not to tell anyone . . .'

'Promise!' cry three voices in unison.

I take a deep breath, my cheeks aflame. 'He'd just told everyone in the team that he fancied me. Fancied Elle, I mean. Now he can't look me in the face.'

'Aaah!' says Ali.

'Poor Marvyn,' says Tash.

'OHHHHHHH!!' Lissa's wails drown them out. 'It's not fair! Everyone I like fancies someone else. Ajay is mad about Tash and now Marvyn fancies you.'

'Not any more, he doesn't. Anyway, listen: Lofty fancies you!'

'Lofty?'

'The tall one. Mr Little's son.'

We all dissolve into laughter as she goes bright red. But, actually, she looks quite pleased.

'And Ryan likes you, Ali.'

'Ryan?' She smiles and shrugs her shoulders like it's no big deal.

'Who fancies me?' asks Tash.

'*Everyone!*' we all say and Tash laughs with delight.

'I like Ajay best,' she admits. 'Who do you like best, Ali? Ryan or Austen?'

'Austen, of course,' she says. 'But not in that way!' she adds hastily.

Who do I like best? Marvyn or Rupert? Rupert, definitely.

I sigh deeply. I'm feeling really happy today. It's like a cloud has lifted from over my head. I can be honest and open with my three best mates at last. That's really important to me. Because, although we're all having a giggle about boys, it's my girl mates that matter to me most.

Plus I've had a good chat with my dad. We all have. We sat round the table in our kitchen on Saturday night after the matches – Mum, Dad, Gran, Jade and me – and we talked about all the things we should've talked about a long time ago. All the things that had been left unsaid. And Mum and Dad both admitted they'd made mistakes in the way they'd handled things over the divorce and agreed that Dad would see far more of us in the future.

You never know, we might even start going to see West Park Wanderers again.

When I've got time, that is.

I'm mean, I'm pretty busy these days, what with playing top-class football and hockey . . .

And hanging out with the rest of the amazing Secrets Club, of course.

No More
Secrets

The Secrets Club

Alice's and Tash's secrets are out.
Now Dani's secret is revealed too.
The friends have promised
NO MORE SECRETS!
But can they keep to it?

Are YOU in the Secrets Club? Join up at
www.secretsclubbooks.com

Bright and shiny and sizzling with fun stuff . . .

puffin.co.uk

WEB FUN

UNIQUE and exclusive digital content!
Podcasts, photos, Q&A, Day in the Life of, interviews
and much more, from Eoin Colfer, Cathy Cassidy,
Allan Ahlberg and Meg Rosoff to Lynley Dodd!

WEB NEWS

The **Puffin Blog** is packed with posts and photos from
Puffin HQ and special guest bloggers. You can also sign up
to our monthly newsletter **Puffin Beak Speak**

WEB CHAT

Discover something new EVERY month –
books, competitions and treats galore

WEBBED FEET

(Puffins have funny little feet and
brightly coloured beaks)

Point your mouse our way today!

It all started with a Scarecrow

Puffin is over seventy years old.
Sounds ancient, doesn't it? But Puffin has never been
so lively. We're always on the lookout for the next big
idea, which is how it began all those years ago.

Penguin Books was a big idea from the mind of
a man called Allen Lane, who in 1935 invented
the quality paperback and changed the world.
**And from great Penguins, great Puffins grew,
changing the face of children's books forever.**

The first four Puffin Picture Books were hatched in 1940 and the
first Puffin story book featured a man with broomstick arms called
Worzel Gummidge. In 1967 Kaye Webb, Puffin Editor, started the
Puffin Club, promising to **'make children into readers'**.
She kept that promise and over 200,000 children became devoted
Puffineers through their quarterly instalments of *Puffin Post*.

Many years from now, we hope you'll look back and
remember Puffin with a smile. **No matter what your age
or what you're into, there's a Puffin for everyone.**
The possibilities are endless, but one thing is for sure:
whether it's a picture book or a paperback, a sticker book
or a hardback, **if it's got that little Puffin
on it – it's bound to be good.**